CASE OF THE
ONE-EYED TIGER

CASE OF THE ONE-EYED TIGER

J.M. POOLE

W🌐RLDWIDE

TORONTO • NEW YORK • LONDON
AMSTERDAM • PARIS • SYDNEY • HAMBURG
STOCKHOLM • ATHENS • TOKYO • MILAN
MADRID • WARSAW • BUDAPEST • AUCKLAND

For my father, Jim…

Life has recently thrown you some curve balls. While not pleasant, and I certainly wouldn't wish it on my worst enemy, I do believe it has been for the best. I'm hoping certain parts of this book will make you smile. Trust me, you'll know what I mean when you get there. :)

WORLDWIDE™

ISBN-13: 978-1-335-90110-1

Case of the One-Eyed Tiger

First published in 2016 by J.M. Poole.
Reprinted in 2020 by Secret Staircase Books, an imprint of Columbine Publishing Group, LLC.
This edition published in 2023 with revised text.

For questions and comments about the quality of this book, please contact us at CustomerService@Harlequin.com.

Harlequin Enterprises ULC
22 Adelaide St. West, 41st Floor
Toronto, Ontario M5H 4E3, Canada
www.ReaderService.com

Printed in U.S.A.

ACKNOWLEDGMENTS

This book would not be here without the help of a number of people. First and foremost, my wife, Giliane. I never would have imagined what was necessary when building your own fictional town. We spent many late night sessions dreaming up what a town needs, where it should be found on a map, who runs it, and so on. You have my eternal love, babe!

I must also thank my beta readers. Diane, Deb, Jason, Laura, Barb, Caroline, Sorcha, and Michelle—thank you for volunteering your time. Your amazing abilities in locating typos, grammatical errors, plot holes, and so on provide a valuable resource I plan on continuing to use just as much as I can. :)

And I must acknowledge you, the reader. Thank you for giving my first foray into the mystery genre a try. I hope you like it!

ONE

THIS HAD TO be a record.

What the heck happened? How did I end up in this mess? For crying out loud, I just moved here. Tell you what, let's do a recap, shall we? In less than twenty-four hours I had managed to alienate family members I never knew I had, run afoul of the local cops, AND land my sorry rear end in jail accused of—you'll love this—theft and murder. Oh, I mustn't forget that my name is now on a set of adoption papers making me the legal guardian and owner of...

You know what? I'm getting ahead of myself. Let me start from the beginning.

My name is Zachary Anderson. Zack to my friends. I'm forty-three, six feet tall, have brown hair (with more gray than I care to admit), blue eyes, and I'm reasonably built (especially for someone my age). How? I have a date with my elliptical five nights a week, which I have learned I really shouldn't miss.

Why would you care about how I look? The short answer is, you don't. So why bother telling you? Because it's my story and it helps set the scene. I could go into details, but you really don't care to hear about that. Besides, I have a nasty habit of veering off topic. I'll try to keep it under control.

As I was saying, I try to keep myself in good shape.

Not only for myself, but for Samantha as well. At least, I used to.

My darling Samantha. We had been childhood sweethearts. We married right out of high school, much to our family's chagrin. My own mother decided the marriage would never last, seeing how both Samantha and I were incredibly strong willed. Over twenty years later our marriage was still going strong. We lasted well past our family's expectations and then some. Nobody gave us a chance, but we made it. Siblings, friends, even my own parents' marriages crumbled in front of our eyes. Not us. Our love for each other was special. Unique.

Six months ago, in less time than it takes to say "I told you so", Samantha's SUV unexpectedly swerved into oncoming traffic and collided head-on with a semi, effectively ending the utopia we had created together. The stink of it was no one could find a reason why. Had Samantha lost control of her car? Had she suffered some type of medical trauma? A seizure, maybe? The investigators were beside themselves trying to figure out what had happened. It was the only logical explanation, they said. The problem with that line of thinking was Samantha had been in perfect health.

Before you suggest mechanical problems, I know it wasn't her SUV. I had just bought her that car two months prior to the accident. It had been running perfectly. Had the detectives been able to examine it, they would have backed me up on that. However, there hadn't been anything recognizable left after the collision.

Yes, the wreck was that bad. Thankfully, I was told Samantha had been killed instantly. More than likely she never knew what had hit her.

With a heavy heart I packed up our house and sold

it, along with ninety-five percent of the contents, just as soon as I was able to function again. I had to get out of there. Everything reminded me of Samantha, and the last thing I wanted to do was fall back into a funk. I needed a change of scenery. I had planned on finding a quiet corner of the desert to bury myself in my work when…

Oh. I should mention what I do. I'm a self-employed writer. A storyteller. Before I tell you what kind, however, I should warn you that you'll probably be surprised. Really. When I tell you, don't laugh, and don't judge me.

I'm a romance writer. I, uh, discovered I have a knack for writing them, the real steamy kind. Before you jump to any conclusions, I'm not the typical back room writer of dirty books. I am a legitimate author just trying to make a living, so get your mind out of the gutter. These are genuine, R-rated stories that appeal to men just as much as they appeal to women. I know. Much to my dismay I've had just as many male fans write to me as I've had female fans.

I learned that romance readers were voracious and snapped up anything that had an attractive, scantily clad couple on the cover. They'd preorder the next book in the series before even finishing the one they were presently reading. That was the type of market I wanted as my readers.

It's not something I'm proud of, but the pay is good. So good that it enables me to stay self-employed and set my own hours. I just don't volunteer any specifics about my profession. The last thing I want to admit is that behind a computer, I'm known as Chastity Wadsworth.

I can't have it known that a guy, and a boring, normal

guy such as myself, was the person behind that outland-ish pseudonym. So that's why I chose an exotic nom de plume to pen all my romance novels. The steamier the overall image, the more sales they tend to make.

I said, no laughing.

Ah. I can just hear you now. You're wondering what Samantha thought of this unusual profession. Would you be surprised to learn she thought it was hysterical? She encouraged me to make the books just as steamy as they could be without pushing them into mainstream erotica.

Trust me, guys, when you're an author, and your wife suggests making your novels as sensual as they could be, it can only be a good thing. Our lives were perfect. Until that damn day when…

Sorry. See what I did there? I saw the tangent com-ing and veered back on track. You're welcome.

Back to the story. I was feeling depressed. I lacked motivation. Inspiration. My novels reflected that. As a result, for the first time ever, my sales began to drop. After a few months I had become desperate to reverse the worrying trend. The problem was, I knew what was dragging me down. Samantha's death. However, that wasn't something I could quickly bounce back from. I challenge you to lose a spouse and see how great you feel about it.

Thankfully, that's when news came that would for-ever change my life. Whether or not it's for the best has yet to be determined.

I received a letter from some attorney I didn't know, living in a city I've never heard of, telling me that due to Samantha's death, I had become the sole beneficiary of a large estate that included a private winery in south-western Oregon. I had to ask the attorney if he had the right guy. As far as I was aware, neither Samantha nor I had any ties to the Pacific Northwest.

As it turns out, I was wrong. You'll soon see that I'm wrong quite often. Anyway, my wife had a great aunt living up there, and as fortune would have it, the old lady had passed away. Great Aunt Bonnie had left her estate not to her kids, which is what I would have expected, but to us. Specifically, the two of us. I had thought the request was odd, but the attorney assured me he had his facts straight. Apparently, Aunt Bonnie had been adamant. Samantha and I were specifically named as the only two she wanted to leave her estate to. Why? I don't know. I suppose I'll never know. Unfortunately, thanks to Samantha's accident, I was it.

So I had a choice to make. After months of sluggish book sales, with numerous reviewers telling me I had lost my unique edge, I could either try to reinvent myself in the deserts of Phoenix, or I could pull up stakes and move north for a complete change of scenery. With no ties left in Arizona, and no desire to be constantly reminded of my wife's tragic demise, the decision was an easy one. I moved.

If I had known then what I know now, I would have reconsidered my decision to move to the Pacific Northwest.

MY FIRST DAY as an Oregonian started as you would have expected. It was raining. It was raining when I crossed into Oregon, and it has been pretty much raining ever since with only brief patches of sunshine. Grumbling, I checked the forecast. Guess what? There was a one-hundred-percent chance it was going to rain tonight, tomorrow, and for the next ten days. Guess I should've checked the Weather Channel to see what I was getting myself into. Apparently, there's a reason why the Pacific Northwest stays so green. The amount of rainfall Oregon receives is in no way exaggerated.

Thankfully I didn't have to lift a finger to move my stuff. Not only did I not bring much with me—the attorney had indicated that the house I had inherited was fully furnished—but I had also hired movers. I had a great time sitting on my rear playing traffic cop for a bunch of guys that were bigger than me.

Oh, yeah. I guess I should have mentioned this, as if you couldn't figure it out based on my chosen profession. I'm lazy. I could afford the movers, so why not have someone else do all the work? I'll bet the company never had to haul such a small load across that many states before.

Hey, I'm paying your bill. You may put that box over there, please.

I hadn't even had a chance to go through the sprawling house yet, let alone unpack the small stack of boxes the men had deposited in one of the bedrooms, when my day started to turn for the worst. Everything happened so fast. The attorney had met me at the house at the same time the movers had arrived. He had me sign a stack of paperwork and then dropped a ring of keys into my hand. Thirty minutes later, I was telling the guys where to put all my crap.

I had just watched the moving van drive away when the phone rang. Answering it gave me a welcome surprise. It was the last voice I had ever expected to hear in Pomme Valley, Oregon.

"Zack! What's up, bro? Is it really you? Did you really move to Pomme Valley?"

"Who is this?"

"It's Harry!"

"Harry? Harry Watt? You're kidding! You're in Pomme Valley, too? What are the odds the two of us would end up in the same dinky town?"

Harrison Watt had been a classmate of mine during my second set of high school years. I guess I should explain. No, I didn't flunk out and repeat any years. I had attended school in the same school district from second grade all the way through the tenth. However, as luck would have it, I had been forced to move away and therefore attend a new high school for my junior and senior years. Harry had been part of the group of friends I had hung out with after the move. What he was doing all the way over here, in the same Podunk little town that I had moved to, was beyond me. As long as I had him on the phone, I guess I should ask a few questions, huh?

"How long have you been living out here, Harry?"

"Five years now. I love it out here."

"How did you even know I was here? I literally just watched the movers drive their truck away. I haven't unpacked or anything. How'd you get my number?"

"First rule of living in a small town. Get used to the fact that everyone knows everything about you."

"Well, that's…unsettling. What in the world possessed you to move out here, Harry?"

"I might ask you the same question, pal. As for me, I'm a respectable part of the community now. Can you believe it?"

Absolutely not. Harry was the biggest troublemaker I had ever met. Stolen street signs, borrowing cars without permission, petty theft, you name it, he did it. In fact, now that I think about it, not once did I ever hear about him landing in jail or even getting questioned by the police. I had always assumed he had some sort of inside connection at the police department. Turns out I was right. You'll find out how in just a little bit.

"Not in a million years, pal."

"You ought to stop by so we can catch up. We can grab a bite to eat. Whataya say?"

"Sure. Just remember I'm new to town and haven't a clue where everything is yet. Where would you like to meet?"

"Why don't you stop by my office?"

"You say that as though I know where you are."

"I'm on the corner of Main and 5th."

"How about some directions?"

"Get with the times! Don't you have a smartphone? Tell it to give you directions."

I had a smartphone, only it was smarter than I was. I missed my old flip phone.

"No problem. I'll find you. I want to check out the town anyway."

"You weren't kidding, were you? Is this your first day here? You're going to love this town. See you in, what, an hour?"

My sense of direction was terrible. I needed some time to check out the area.

"Why don't we make it noon? I've got to open an account at the bank, set up the utilities, pray that this town has a faster internet connection than dial-up, and run a few other errands. It'll give me some time."

"Sounds great, pal. I'll have Julie meet us there. She has her lunch hour at noon."

"Julie?"

"Yeah, my wife. Didn't I tell you I was married?"

"You? You're kidding! I seem to recall you swearing off relationships after Tami Bowen dumped you."

"Ah. Tami. I had forgotten about her. Just do me a favor. When you meet Julie? Try not to bring up anything that might make me look bad. My wife hasn't even touched the tip of the iceberg when it comes to my youth."

Lunch was starting to look up.

"Sure thing." I crossed my fingers. Harry had embarrassed me on more than one occasion. I smelled payback. "Whatever you say."

While I'm hopelessly navigating through this quaint little town, looking for City Hall, a grocery store, a pizza joint, and several other businesses that were on my "must find" list, I should tell you what the internet taught me about Pomme Valley. Or PV, as the locals call it.

Less than 3,000 people call PV home. I have to admit that when I saw those numbers after I Googled the city, I almost spewed my drink all over my laptop. It's a small city. A very small city. I'll even go so far as to say that it's a really freakin' small town. There were only two traffic lights in the entire town. I know. I counted 'em. There were more than twice that number of lights just getting from my old house to the gas station back in Phoenix.

Main Street consisted of a neat row of shops on either side of the street. Cute, artsy-fartsy shops were offering any number of bizarre trinkets, woven rugs and blankets, and strange sculptures being passed off as art. In fact, as I drove by the small shop with the bright purple door, I swore I could see crime scene tape forming an

"X" over the door. I chalked it up to some artists wanting to express themselves. Hippies, all of 'em.

I parked my Jeep in a parking lot off of Oregon Street and stepped out into the fresh cool air. The street name had me turning back to see if my eyes were playing tricks on me. Oregon Street? Really? Yep. I had read that right. Not very original, guys.

I figured that if this small town were to have a pizza joint and—please, God—a Chinese restaurant, then I should find them somewhere on this street. Main Street was the busiest road in town and after driving around for a few minutes, I could see why. The clouds had parted, allowing the sun to peek through for a while. As a result, tourists had poured out of nearby buildings and flocked the sidewalks in droves. Senior citizens adorned in Hawaiian shirts, khaki shorts, and sandals (most were wearing socks—if my fashion sense ever stoops to that level you have my permission to shoot me) were wandering up and down the sidewalks. Where had they come from? Look at all of them! They could have only come from...

A large tour bus suddenly appeared and pulled up to an open curb. It blared its horn once and the doors opened. Thank God. It was time for the fashion-challenged to go home.

A new stream of visitors poured out of the bus. Within moments I was fighting a losing battle, trying to swim upstream in a sea of people moving in the opposite direction, anxious to get where they're going before it started raining again. Fed up with the massive amounts of tourists, I ducked into the closest shop.

My stomach growled as my nose reported in; it had approved of my choice of businesses. I had just stepped into some type of coffee shop. While not a fan of coffee, my nose easily picked up the scents of pastries, baked goods, and something that smelled like homemade soup. I glanced at the sign on the window. Wired Coffee & Café. Cute. If I bought something then I could hang out in here to see if the mass of people subsided. I winced as I caught a whiff of freshly brewed coffee. I could only hope they offered coffee-free drinks.

"What can I get for you today?" a bright, perky girl asked. Her smile brought out her dimples, which gave her a girl-next-door look. She also looked to be no older than sixteen.

"Do you sell soda here?"

The young girl blinked at me a few times before her head swiveled to look at a point behind me. I turned to look and saw one of those new-fangled soda machines that could produce hundreds, if not thousands, of flavor varieties. I really shouldn't order anything else since I would be grabbing lunch with Harry, but those bagels looked fresh and appealing. A snack certainly wouldn't hurt anything.

"Roger that. I'll have a large soda, please. Hmm, you know what? That pumpkin bagel looks good. I'll take that, too."

The teen smiled. "Of course. What kind of cream cheese would you like? We have mixed berry, chive and onion, salmon, and honey."

"Salmon? Seriously?"

The girl reached under the counter and grabbed a plastic container. She pulled the lid off, revealing a mass of whipped pink goo inside. She reached for a spatula and was ready to dip it in the nasty looking mess when I finally regained my wits.

"Whoa. Wait. No salmon. I didn't even know they made that flavor."

The girl replaced the tub and looked expectantly at me, spatula held at the ready.

"Um, don't you have plain?"

The girl seemed confused.

"Plain? Sure, I guess. I don't get many requests for that. Let me look."

As soon as she finished slathering on a layer of cream cheese that had to be an inch thick, the girl rang me up, handed me an empty cup and a small paper plate with my bagel. I made my selection from the complicated soda machine and sat down at the nearest empty table.

Don't judge. I know what you're thinking. I happen to like bagels with cream cheese, washed down with a cool, refreshing soda. I never said I was a health nut.

"Sure are a lot of 'em out there," a voice commented from my right.

I turned to see a guy younger than me wearing wire rim glasses, a blue long-sleeved, button-down shirt, jeans, and black sneakers. Some type of tablet was sitting on a magazine directly in front of him. He was casually sitting at the table next to me drinking some type of coffee-laden drink that probably had six different names to it judging by the number of letters the girl had written on the cup.

"I'll say. Listen, what's the deal? I saw a bus outside dropping them off. What's going on?"

Just then we both heard what sounded like a semi-truck releasing the pressure in its air brakes. Shocked, I turned to inspect the surroundings. The stranger studied me as though I was the one responsible, which I wasn't. That's when I heard a chorus of giggles coming from behind me. The stranger and I turned to see a table full of red-faced women. They were all wearing identical purple floppy hats.

"Yikes," I mumbled. "Lay off the bran, ladies."

The stranger slapped a hand over his face and quickly faced forward. He looked at me and grinned.

"Are you visiting?"

"Actually, no. I just moved here earlier today. I haven't even finished unpacking yet."

The guy nodded. "Ah. You'd be the one who moved into the Davies place. You're the new owner of Lentari Cellars, aren't you?"

"Lentari Cellars?"

"Seriously? You didn't know?"

I frowned.

"I haven't had time to go through the papers the attorney gave me, if that's what you're asking."

The guy held out a hand.

"Spencer Woodson. You can call me Woody. Everyone does."

I shook Woody's hand.

"Zack Anderson. Nice to meet you, Woody. How did you know I just moved here?"

"This is a small town. We get lots of visitors but few regulars. When Ms. Davies died earlier this year everyone wondered what would happen to the winery and her estate. Everyone assumed that there'd be a big auction and the estate would be broken up. I guess we were all wrong."

"Sorry, there won't be any auctions," I confirmed. "Ms. Davies was my late wife's great aunt, so that makes her family. I wouldn't feel comfortable selling her things."

"Did you know the estate came with its own winery?"

"I knew about the winery," I admitted. "However, I had never heard what it was called. Lentari Cellars. Has a nice ring to it."

"They produced the best Syrah I have ever tasted," Woody told me, with a grin.

"What is shurraw?"

"Syrah. It's a type of red wine oftentimes made with black berries or black currants."

"You know a lot about wine," I said.

"Everyone in town does," Woody said, taking another sip from his cup. "Pomme Valley may be known for our apple farms but coming in a close second would be our wines. Let me guess. You're not a wine lover."

"I can't stand it," I admitted.

"You moved to the wrong place, my friend," Woody said. "Don't you see all those people out there? They're here for the annual wine tasting festival. Free booze. Why do you think they were all bused in?"

"They're all here to drink wine?" I asked, amazed.

Wine. Ugh. Why'd it have to be wine? I can't stand the stuff. I'd rather drink a huge glass of prune juice, and don't get me started with that nasty crap.

"You really don't like wine?" Woody asked, taking a long sip from his tall paper cup. Clearly my non-wine drinking kind is in the minority here.

"Not at all."

"Yet you moved here knowing you had inherited a winery."

"I didn't know the whole town was a bunch of connoisseurs," I protested.

Woody grinned. "Not all of us are. So, are you going to sell it?"

"What? The winery? Why, do you want to buy it?"

"Not me, no thanks. I already have a business. I own and operate Toy Closet just down the street."

"You sell toys?"

"Think of it like a hobby shop. I stock model trains, rocket engines, and even some old D&D stuff."

"D&D?"

"Yeah, you know. Dungeons & Dragons. My parents played it when they were kids."

Jesus. I had played it when I was a kid. That meant I'm old enough to be this kid's father. How depressing was that?

"So, um, are there people who still play?"

Woody nodded. "There are entire communities out there that live and breathe D&D. If they're willing to buy then I'm willing to stock."

"Wait. Are you telling me that there are people in Pomme Valley who actually play D&D?"

"Of course. I'm Dungeon Master of our local chapter. If you ever want to get involved, let me know. I'll get you a seat at our next game."

When pigs fly, pal.

"Yeah, okay. Thanks. I'll let you know."

"Did you hear all those sirens earlier?"

My ears perked up. Sirens? I hadn't heard any sirens, had I?

"No. What happened?"

"Poor Zora."

I took a sip of my raspberry lemon-lime vanilla soda and glanced once more at the passing crowds.

"Who's Zora?"

"Zora Lumen owns 4th Street Gallery. She's a little strange, like not all lights are on upstairs, if you know what I mean."

Sure I did. There are people like that everywhere. Every family had at least one pear in the apple barrel. Come to think of it, mine had two.

"Yeah, I know what you mean. What about her?"

"Her place was robbed and her assistant was killed!"

"What? Here? You're kidding! That's the last thing I would expect to happen around these parts. Wait. Does her gallery have a purple door?"

Woody nodded. "Yep. A very garish purple door, if you ask me. Then again, no one really understands Zora's style." He shook his head, pushed his thin silver glasses up the bridge of his nose, and scratched at his goatee. "This is the first murder PV has seen in over fifty years!"

"When did this happen?" I wanted to know. Had it been today? Last night? What was stolen? I guess I should be asking my new friend those questions, right? "You said her place was robbed. Any idea what was taken?"

Woody nodded. "They're calling it PV's crime of the century. Emelie Vång's newest, most dazzling object d'art was in the gallery and it was stolen. Maybe you've heard of it. It's called *Bengál*."

Great. He's talking about art. There's a subject that I know next to nothing about. Someone must have really wanted to... Wait. Emelie Vång? I stand corrected. I had heard of her. She's the Swedish glass artist that's taken the world by storm this past year. I've even seen a couple of her pieces. Weird, abstract blobs of glass with intense swirls of color nestled within its heart. Wow.

Listen to me, huh? For a second there I sounded like I knew what I was talking about.

But, I shouldn't lose focus. Back to the problem at hand. Did you hear what Woody had said? Someone had been murdered there. Leave it to me to bring a piece of Phoenix's violence to Small Town, USA.

So, some piece of glass was stolen. Why? How long had it been here? Better yet, why would a world-famous artist have ties with a local art gallery here in Nowhere-ville, Oregon? Had this *Bengál* thing been on display? Why hadn't it been stored more securely?

It didn't add up.

"You okay?" Woody asked as he tipped back his cup to finish off his drink.

Whoops. I was caught zoning. Again.

I nodded. "Yeah, I'm fine. This Bengal thing that was stolen..."

"*Bengál*," Woody interrupted, once more adding emphasis on the second syllable.

"Whatever. What's it look like? How big is it?"

"It's a tiger."

I let out a snort.

"Thanks, Captain Obvious. Can you give me anything more than that?"

In response, Woody pulled out his phone, tapped the screen a couple of times, and then handed it to me. There, on the screen, was a picture of *Bengál*. It was an ugly thing. Not one of Ms. Vång's better works, if you ask me.

Conveniently enough, someone had laid a yard-stick next to the glass sculpture in the picture. It was 38 inches long and about 20 inches high at its highest point. The tiger was in a crouch, as though it was ready to pounce on some hapless prey. The body was mostly clear, as though I was looking at pure water, but I could also see that some coloring had been added, giving it a faint purplish hue. The tiger's front legs, however, were a slightly different color. Instead of purple I could see an orange-reddish coloring. Like burnt cinnamon.

I snorted derisively. Burnt cinnamon? Where had that come from?

The tiger's rear legs were faint blue. I couldn't see any black stripes anywhere, but I did see how the surface of the sculpture was wavy, rippled. It definitely gave the tiger the appearance of having stripes without having any black color anywhere on the piece.

The more I stared at the piece, the more it grew on me.

"Wonderful, isn't it?" Woody asked. "I didn't like it at first but the more I see it, the more I like it. I just wish whoever took it would put it back."

Woody took his phone back, swiped his finger across the screen, and returned it to me. A new image appeared. This was a close up of the tiger's head. The first thing I noticed was the tiger only had one eye. The other eye, the one that was there, looked an awful lot like a ruby, leading me to believe the other eye had been pried loose and stolen.

"You're wondering about the eye, right?" Woody asked. "Everyone does. Ms. Vång insists the tiger has the other eye squeezed shut."

"She insists?" I repeated, frowning. "You're saying you've talked to her?"

"Of course. She visits PV often."

"Why? Does she live here?"

Woody shrugged. "I don't know. She's supposed to

be Swedish so I would have assumed she lives in Sweden. As far as PV is concerned, everyone has speculated on Emelie's connection, and how she knows Zora, but no one really knows."

The owner of Toy Closet pushed back from his table and gathered his things, namely the tablet and the magazine.

"Back to the salt mines. Wish me luck. Hey, if you really are going to sell Lentari Cellars, I know several people that would probably be interested."

"Thanks. I'll keep that in mind."

I didn't know what to make of that. Someone wanted the winery? The analytical portion of my brain made a mental note to research old Aunt Bonnie's winery to see if there was some hidden value somewhere I didn't know about. I watched Woody leave and decided I should be on my way, too.

I found the bank, opened all the necessary accounts, and found out from the teller that the city's utilities were all handled by City Hall. Naturally it was on the other side of town. I guess I shouldn't complain. I probably could have walked there. In fact, you know what? Judging by the number of people milling about and crossing the street wherever they felt like it, it'd probably be safer if I didn't drive. Besides, it was time to find Harry's office. This was a small town. I should be able to find it without any problems.

Wait. His office? What did he do, anyway? Had he said? I shook my head. I couldn't remember. Oh, well. Guess I'll find out soon enough.

"Excuse me," I said as I put my ID and all other necessary cards back into my wallet, "but do you have any idea where I might find the offices of Harry Watt?"

The teller blinked at me a few times.

"Harry Watt? Dr. Harrison Watt, the vet?"

I'm sure my eyebrows just shot up.

"Doctor? Harry? You're kidding."

"He's been the only veterinarian in town for several years now, ever since Doctor Ruckman retired."

Harry was a doctor? Unbelievable. Apparently, the teller must have sensed my skepticism.

"He's a very good vet. Do you know Doctor Watt?"

"I do. He's an old friend from high school."

"Oh! He told me about his twenty-five-year reunion coming up. You must be so excited!"

Age jokes. Why do I always get hit with the age jokes? I don't look that old, do I? Punk teeny bopper.

"Dr. Watt's clinic is just down the street on the right. It's on the corner of Main and 5th. That road right out there is 3rd. It's two blocks over."

I thanked the snarky teller and waded my way back into the throng of people milling about outside. I longingly looked back in the direction of where I had parked my Jeep and briefly considered going back for it. Just then the traffic light at the corner turned green and a whole mess of people hurried across. In both directions. There were so many people that they didn't fit within the painted lines on the crosswalk and therefore spilled over.

I wasn't about to try and drive in this chaos. I'd just have to suck it up and walk.

I found myself outside the building at the corner of 5th St. and Main just before noon. I looked at the single story professional office that sat on the corner. It had a large chain link fence—my first clue that I should never have stepped foot through that accursed door—

wrapped around the perimeter of the property and then I saw several more sections of fence further dividing up the yard. Each narrow section had strips of grass, a small house, and a large water bowl.

Again, I know you've figured out what you're looking at, but for me, sadly, it took a little while. I glanced at the outdoor kennels and didn't think anything of it. He was the vet, wasn't he? Maybe he wanted to provide the recovering dogs a place to enjoy the fresh air. Outside.

Yeah, you're right. I was stupid. Not one of my better days.

I gazed at the sign, which read Watt's Vet Clinic & Animal Shelter. I shook my head in amazement. It was true. Harry was a vet. No matter what his credentials were, there was no way I was calling him "Doc". My poor brain was already short circuiting just thinking about Harry in his new role. In a white doctor's coat.

I strode into the clinic and immediately looked around. While clean in appearance, there was no mistaking the telltale smell of a strong disinfectant. I can only imagine that something bad must've just happened in here. Thankfully, it had already been cleaned up. But, that didn't stop me from automatically checking the bottom of my shoes.

Good. Nothing there.

"Good afternoon," a woman cheerfully told me. "How can I help you today?"

She was about my age, tall (for a woman—about five-foot-nine), and had short brown hair.

"I'm looking for Harry Watt," I announced.

"Of course. You must be the friend of his he told us about. Are you Zack?"

I nodded. "Guilty as charged."

"He told me to send you back to his office. It's right through that door there and it'll be at the end of the hall. It'll be the only door you see."

"Perfect. Thanks."

I opened the door and froze in my tracks. My mind flashed back to the "Animal Rescue" part of Harry's sign and groaned. That sneaky jerk. The back part of Harry's clinic was where he kenneled all the dogs waiting to be adopted. The dogs were all lined up, in perfect military precision, as if they were in the middle of an inspection. They were sitting in straight lines on either side of the aisle and were staring straight at me.

Okay, I don't know about you, but it's been my understanding that most people will actively avoid visiting the pound, or any type of place where they adopt animals, because one look at the helpless dogs staring—imploring—at you to look into their eyes will melt even the coldest hearts imaginable. If I looked at any of these dogs, then I just knew I'd end up adopting one of them. It's in my nature. I've always liked dogs, only I've never owned one. So, I needed to walk forward, keep my head down, and ignore everything around me.

I could smell the dogs, and I had to admit, Harry ran a clean clinic. I couldn't smell any traces of dog poo back there, but I could smell the dogs themselves. While not really offensive, I could tell that several of them could use a bath.

A collar jingled alarmingly close. Another dog yipped excitedly. I almost looked up at that one. My eyes narrowed to slits. I was practically squinting. I was almost to the door! One quick turn of the knob and I'd be home free!

Movement in my peripheral vision attracted my attention. I could tell that a dog had just appeared and was now watching me. Don't ask me how I knew, I just did. I could feel those two canine eyeballs boring through the back of my skull.

Then I heard it. An unmistakable sigh, and it had come from the dog that had just appeared. Once more the rules flashed through my mind:

1. Don't move your eyes from the floor.
2. Don't make eye contact.
3. Under no circumstances should you ever, EVER pet the dog.

Break the rules and presto, you'll find yourself with a new roommate. Well, I didn't need a dog and I didn't want a dog, so it's eyes on the floor for me. However, that sigh had sounded so human! It spoke volumes. That sigh said the poor fellow wanted a permanent home and had resigned himself to never having one.

I couldn't help it. The move was automatic; reflexive. I looked.

The owner of that sigh was a breed of dog I had only seen on dog shows, not that I watched many dog shows. It was a short, squat little fellow with an elongated body, short, stumpy legs, and no tail. The ears were small, erect, and tapered to a rounded point. The fur was thick and luxurious, but not long, and consisted of a beautiful mix of black, orange, and white.

Beautiful? Did I just call a dog beautiful? Dang! No. No. I will not like you, dog. Keep your charms to yourself, do you hear me?

So what kind of breed was he, I wondered. I know I've seen pictures of them before. But from where?

A picture of the Queen of England flashed through my brain. The Queen! This was her favorite breed of dog. Now I knew what this little fellow was: a corgi.

The corgi approached the other side of the chain link fence, plopped his rump down onto the concrete floor, looked up at me, and lifted a foreleg in greeting. Before I knew what I was doing, I had squatted down and was holding a hand up to the fence. A warm, wet tongue flicked once across my open palm.

I groaned. I was in trouble. The corgi had dark brown eyes with gold flecks in them and had locked both those eyes directly onto mine. For several seconds neither of us moved a muscle. Finally, when I ended up blinking, the dog rose to its feet and panted at me, looking for all the world like he was smiling. Then I heard a chuckle. I looked up to see Harry grinning at me from his open doorway.

My friend had definitely aged, as I'm sure I had in his eyes. He had an unmistakable paunch, which I'm guessing was brought on by one too many beers. He had thinning hair and was sporting a full beard. He was also holding a clipboard with a set of papers on it.

"No."

"An excellent choice, pal. You and he are going to be the best of friends."

"Harry, no. I don't need a dog."

"But he needs a human. He's picked you."

"I don't know anything about caring for a dog! Are you kidding me? You can't do this to me, Harry."

"It's easy," my friend assured me. "Feed him, take

him on walks, and make sure he has plenty of fresh, clean water. That's it."

"There's more to caring for a dog than that, pal," I mumbled as I started filling out the necessary adoption forms.

I handed the clipboard back to Harry, who gave them a quick once over. He unclipped a leash from a whole row of them hanging nearby and opened the corgi's kennel. As soon as the dog was secured, Harry turned to me and held out the end of the leash, as though he was presenting me keys to the city.

"Zack, meet Sherlock. Sherlock, meet your new daddy."

TWO

I TOOK THE leash and looked down at my new ward. Sherlock, for his part, had to bend his neck up at almost a ninety-degree angle so he could look all the way up at me. I leaned down to give the dog a quick pat on his head. As if that one act cemented the deal, Sherlock pulled on his leash, clearly anxious to get out of jail.

"Ready for some lunch?" Harry companionably asked as he followed me back to the clinic's lobby. Sherlock's doggy toenails clicked loudly across the concrete floor.

"You just suckered me into adopting a dog. Where are we supposed to go for lunch? I can't just leave him in my car."

Harry smiled. He took off his white doctor's coat and draped it over the front counter as he walked by.

"Good for you. You're already well on your way to becoming a good dog owner. Never leave your pet unattended in a vehicle."

I stared at Harry, wondering what his life experiences must have been like in order to pull him away from a life destined to land him behind bars. He had transformed himself from a dedicated loser to a responsible veterinarian who was now praising me for caring about Sherlock's well-being.

"Back in an hour, Laura," Harry called back to his receptionist. He held the door open for the two of us.

"As for lunch, you'd be surprised. This whole town is very pet friendly. I thought we could go to Casa de Joe's."

"Casa de Joe's? Dude, tell me you made that up."

We exited the clinic and stepped out into the bright autumn day. Sherlock came to a stop as the two of us stopped by the side of the street.

"I kid you not, pal," Harry laughed, sounding more like the person I knew from school. "They have the best Mexican food in town. Where'd you park?"

I pointed back toward the other side of town.

"Down thataway. I've been walking everywhere. There's too many people crossing the street wherever they feel like it to risk driving."

Harry nodded knowingly.

"Right. I forgot about the wine festival. It's the start of Oscar's night for small wineries around here."

"Huh?" I asked, confused.

"The wine festival is a chance for the local wineries to compete for awards, recognition, that kind of thing," Harry explained.

I whistled. "How many could there be in one small town? There can't be that many, can there?"

Harry grinned. "Guess."

"Five."

"Higher."

"Ten?"

"Higher."

"Fifteen? Come on, man. There's no way."

"Try twenty-four."

"I never imagined such a small town could have that many."

"You'd be surprised," Harry said. "You don't have to

own a vineyard to be considered a winery. Many wineries buy their grapes from local farmers. I know quite a few people who have converted their basements into micro-wineries." He pointed at a pastel blue mini-van. "That baby is mine, right there."

I snorted with disbelief, "A minivan? Why not get a truck to haul around your dogs? I assume that's what you have, right?"

Harry slid open the passenger door and indicated the passenger seats. There was a child's seat strapped to one of the chairs.

"You're kidding."

Harry smiled wildly at me.

"Nope! I got two kids, man. How about you?"

"Samantha and I didn't have any kids," I quietly answered. A dull ache formed in my chest.

A very uncharacteristic Harry zeroed in on my somber mood and was instantly apologetic.

"I'm sorry, bro. What happened?"

"I'll tell you at lunch. Speaking of which," I added, desperate to change the subject, "how is it that the restaurants here don't mind dogs?"

"Because most of the restaurants on Main Street have open terraces. The rules are more lax there. As long as you stay outside the restaurant, owners will allow you to have your dog on the patio. It's the new hip thing. They're calling those terraces 'pet friendly'. You're going to have to help him in," Harry added, looking down at Sherlock, who was looking up at the van and waiting patiently for a "paw" up.

I leaned down to pick up my dog. Sherlock squirmed in my arms, almost causing me to drop him. As I secured my grip on the wiggling corgi, Sherlock managed to twist completely around. Suddenly his head was even with mine. I saw his jaws open. The tongue came out, and I knew what was coming.

The corgi planted a single doggie kiss, right across my face. It must have been Sherlock's way of thanking me for springing him out of jail. I set the appreciative dog in the back of Harry's van and slid the passenger door shut. I climbed into the passenger seat while wiping doggie drool from my face.

"He sure has taken to you," Harry observed. "Sherlock has been kinda standoffish and I was beginning to wonder if he'd ever get adopted. Then you come to town and make a corgi's dream come true."

"I still don't know about this," I told my friend as he pulled out into traffic. "I've never had to care for a dog before. What's he eat? How much should I feed him? Where does he sleep? Is he potty trained?"

"All very good questions," Harry said. "I'll write you a list of notes at lunch that'll cover everything you need to do to properly care for him, okay?"

I had just pulled the seatbelt across my lap and clicked it into place when Harry pulled off Main Street and into the parking lot at Casa de Joe's. We had driven all of one block. I left my hand on my seat belt and stared at Harry.

"Seriously? You drove here when we could have just walked? You know what? I'm pretty sure I've already walked by here today. Twice."

"You're not going to want to walk when you leave here," Harry pointed out. "Besides, I'll drive you and Sherlock back to your car. Think of your dog. Look how short his legs are. A normal walk for you will be a marathon for him."

We exited the van (Sherlock waited patiently to be picked up and set down on the pavement). We walked straight to the open terrace, selected a table, and sat down. Sherlock laid down obediently by my feet, which amazed Harry.

"Are you sure you've never owned a dog before?"

I nodded my head. "Positive."

"He sure seems to like you. Look at that. He's protecting you. That's a very encouraging sign, pal."

"I still feel like I was set up."

Harry shrugged. "That's because you were. It's my responsibility to make sure all the dogs that come to my clinic find their forever homes. Sherlock was adopted once before but was given back several days later. I can't tell you what that does to a dog's spirit."

"Why?" I prompted. "Why was he given back?"

"Incompatibility. Sherlock didn't take to the lady of the house. She didn't like dogs to begin with, but to have Sherlock ignore and disobey her was the final straw, I'm afraid."

"That's too bad."

"It worked out for the best. He has you now."

An attractive woman, whom I'm guessing was in her late thirties, approached. Harry's face broke out into a grin and he quickly stood. He put an arm around the woman's shoulders and turned to me.

"Zack, this is my wife, Julie. Julie, this is Zack. Do you remember him?"

The woman nodded and smiled at me.

"I sure do. It's a pleasure to see you again, Zack! Welcome to our neck of the woods."

Again? I had met her before? Seeing the look of confusion on my face, Harry intervened.

"She graduated from the same high school that we did, only a few years later."

I still didn't remember who this person was. Then again, our old high school in Phoenix had over 1,400 students attending classes. There's no way I could have known them all.

"It's okay if you can't remember," Julie warmly told me. "It was a long time ago."

We all took our seats as the waitress arrived to take our drink order. She left two bowls of tortilla chips and several types of salsa after we placed our orders.

"So did you two get married right out of school?" I asked, curious to see if Harry had followed in my steps.

"No," Harry said. "I should have paid more attention to this pretty girl when we were all students, that's for sure. Turns out Julie's father was the local sheriff. On those rare occasions where we had run-ins with the police, Julie here made certain my name stayed out of it."

I stared incredulously at Harry's wife.

"You? You're the reason Harry stayed out of trouble? How did you pull that off?"

Julie beamed at me.

"I had the biggest crush on Harry in high school. As for my father, well, it was easy. I had my dad wrapped around my little finger when I was young. What can I say? I was, and still am, a daddy's girl. I will admit that there were several times when I had to beg and plead with him to leave poor Harry alone, but in the end, it worked out fine."

I looked at my friend with a look of bewilderment on my face.

"You told me she didn't know about any of the things you did in high school. Obviously, she does. I can't believe you told her about that night at the bowling alley, where we all snuck into the stri—"

"Ose-clay your outh-may!" Harry cried, practically leaping out of his chair and interrupting me mid-sentence. His face had turned beet red and beads of sweat had started forming on his head.

Julie winked at me and smiled conspiratorially at her husband.

"I eak-spay ig-pay atin-lay, oo-tay, ear-day." Julie reached for a chip and dunked it in the bowl of dark red salsa. She smiled again at me. "I think you and I are going to be good friends, Zack. So are you married? Have any kids?"

My face told Julie everything she needed to know before I could even open my mouth. She instantly laid a hand over mine and dropped her voice.

"I'm so sorry. What happened? Can you tell us?"

"This is a subject I don't like talking about 'cause it still hurts, but yeah, I can. Give me a minute." I sighed and took a long swig of my soda. The waitress walked by and, without breaking stride snatched my glass. "You probably knew her, Harry. Samantha Masters. Do you remember her?"

Harry's face lit up.

"Sure, I remember her. Cute short thing that played the flute in the marching band, right? Didn't you go out with her a few times?"

Julie groaned. She moved her hand from mine and placed it over Harry's. And dug in.

"Ouch! Jules, what'd you do that for?"

"Haven't you figured it out yet? He married his high school sweetheart, am I right?"

I nodded. "Yeah, that's right."

Julie kept her talons firmly embedded in her husband's hand and smiled at me.

"Would you please continue?"

"Sam and I married right out of school. We were together for so long that I honestly don't remember what my life was like before her. Anyway, six months ago she was struck head-on in a collision with a semi. She died instantly."

I heard a whine and looked down at my feet. Sherlock had awoken from his nap and jumped up to put his two front feet on my lap. Wow, that dog had a long body.

"Why don't you pick him up?" Harry quietly suggested.

"What? Why?"

"Dogs can sense when their humans are in distress. He knows you're feeling sad. He wants to help."

"You're telling me dogs can sense moods?"

"Oh, yeah," Julie agreed. "My family had a yellow Lab when I was little that always knew when I was feeling sad. She would never leave my side."

I shrugged, hooked my hands under each of Sherlock's squat muscular front legs, and lifted him to my lap. The dog promptly snugged up against my chest and whimpered. He stretched his neck up to lick the underside of my chin.

"I cannot believe this is the same dog," Harry breathed, amazed.

I must have been a sight. Me, a grown man, pining for my dead wife, and cradling a snuggling corgi to my chest. Sitting across the table was an old friend that I realize I didn't know that well anymore and that friend's wife, whom I didn't know at all.

I looked down at the corgi. I didn't know what type

of magic Sherlock used on me but, dang it, I did start to feel better. Coincidence?

"So after the funeral," I continued, giving Sherlock a couple of scratches behind his ears, "I tried to put my life back together there in Phoenix, but just couldn't do it. Everything reminded me of her."

"You needed a change of scenery," Julie guessed.

"I did, yes. Right about that time I was notified that Samantha had a great aunt who had passed away, leaving the two of us her estate."

"Lentari Cellars!" Julie exclaimed. "That's right! You're the new owner! They make the best Gewürztraminer."

The waitress reappeared and presto, my glass of soda was back.

"I heard something similar earlier today," I admitted, grabbing my glass to take another long drink. "Something called 'Syrah', whatever that is."

Julie nodded. "They do make a great Syrah there, too."

"Clearly everybody knows more about wine than I do," I admitted. "I can't stand the stuff."

"But you own a winery now," Harry pointed out. "If you're going to keep the winery then you'd better start learning."

"Yeah, well, we'll see. So what do you do for work, Julie? Harry hasn't said."

"Harry hasn't said a lot of things," she quipped, giving her husband a cryptic smile. "I'm a dispatcher for the PVPD."

"Oh, really? That's very cool. Do you know anything about the murder that happened here?"

Julie leaned forward.

"I should say so. I'm the one who dispatched the crime scene investigators out to the gallery and had to listen as they reported in."

"Can you tell us anything about it?" I pressed, curious.

Just then the waitress reappeared and set out plates of food. She also set a large carafe of soda down in front of me since she had noticed that I had all but drained my glass for the second time. I looked around the table. Julie had ordered some type of burrito, Harry had a set of three enormous enchiladas set before him, and I had ordered a traditional tostada. Just for the record, there was no way I was going to be able to finish this thing off. They must have used an entire head of lettuce for my order and somehow found a tortilla the size of a man-hole cover to set it on.

"I can tell you the investigation is ongoing," Julie continued once the waitress left. "We've been given a number of leads so far, only most haven't panned out."

"And those that have?" Harry asked, around a mouthful of chicken enchilada.

"They say it was an inside job," Julie quietly told us as she sliced another piece off her gargantuan burrito. "The tiger hasn't turned up yet and there are no signs of forced entry, either."

"What about the person who was murdered?" I asked. "Could that be the insider? I think I heard somewhere that the assistant was the one who was killed."

"Right," Julie confirmed, nodding. "Her name was Debra Jacobs. My own personal opinion is that she wasn't the insider, provided this was an inside job."

"Are you sure about that?" Harry asked, lowering his voice. "If anyone had the temperament to try and pull something like this off then I'd definitely say it would be her."

Julie nodded. "Yes, I'm sure. Zora was the only friend Debra had."

"Was she that unsociable?" I said. "Surely there's a reason in there somewhere."

Harry leaned forward and lowered his voice even further.

"Man, that lady was insanely mean. I swear she went out of her way to be as rude as possible."

"She definitely enjoyed creating drama in other people's lives," Julie confirmed. "Put a knife in her hands and she'd stab you in the back with it and not think twice about it."

"Uh, you mean that figuratively, right?" I stammered, concerned.

Julie nodded. "Yes. Of course. Debra was no murderer and she's no thief. I'll agree she was quite difficult, but she wasn't a criminal. I once watched her march a lady back to the cashier stand at the supermarket because she overheard how the customer hadn't been charged for a yogurt."

"Wow," I whistled.

"You made that up," Harry accused. My friend was silent for a moment and then suddenly slapped the table, causing Julie and me to jump in our seats. "Hah! I've got it. There are mirrors in Zora's gallery, aren't there?"

"Mirrors?" Julie repeated as she turned to her husband with a confused look on her face. "What has that got to do with anything?"

"I'll wager she passed by one of them, caught a glimpse of her reflection, and turned herself to stone."

I snorted as Julie giggled. She reached across the table to smack Harry on the arm.

"She was shot, you dork. Besides, don't speak about the dead like that. It's rude."

Harry held up his hands in surrender. "Yeah, well, you laughed."

"You said most leads hadn't panned out," I said to Julie, eager to learn more about the crime. "Have there been any that did?"

Julie nodded. "Just one, I'm afraid."

She then gave me an unsettling look. The hairs on the back of my neck stood up.

"Why are you looking at me like that?" I demanded. "You can't possibly think I had anything to do with this. I wasn't even in town when this happened! At least I don't think I was. Besides, I've never stepped foot inside that gallery."

Harry looked at his wife with concern in his eyes.

"Babe, where are you going with this? Zack didn't do anything. He doesn't have any part of this."

Julie leaned forward again. Both Harry and I did the same.

"From what I hear, the detectives found a couple of clues at the gallery. Clues that point to you, Zack."

"This is nuts," I sputtered, growing angry. "What kind of numbnuts does PV have on its force, anyway? No offense to you, Julie."

"What could they have possibly found, Jules?" Harry wanted to know. "Zack hasn't been in town long enough to leave any traces of anything lying around."

"They wouldn't tell me any specifics," Julie said, dabbing the corner of her mouth with her napkin, "only that they were looking into all possibilities. The last I heard was that they had one working theory, and I'm sure I heard your name in the same sentence, Zack. I'm sorry."

"How would you people even know my name?" I demanded. "I first stepped foot in Pomme Valley earlier today! It's not like there was an official announcement in the paper, right?"

Both Harry and Julie were silent. I swore softly to myself.

"Tell me they didn't."

"Last week," Harry admitted, grinning sheepishly. "There was an article talking about Lentari Cellars and the new owner. You. There wasn't much to tell other than you were moving to town and would be here soon."

"Who told the paper about me?" I demanded, bewildered. "I certainly didn't authorize it."

"Our recycling guy only comes once every two weeks," Julie said. "I'm sure we still have our copy of the paper. I'll get it for you. You definitely bring up a good point."

A shadow fell over our table. Sherlock woofed a warning. I looked up to see an older woman decked out in formal business attire. She was wearing a dark gray overcoat (it had to be seventy outside in the sun!), matching gray skirt, and gray pumps with thick two inch heels. Her silver hair was pulled up into a tight bun and she was wearing dark sunglasses. The woman scowled as she stared down her nose at the three of us.

"Which one of you is Mr. Zachary Anderson?"

I instantly, and I do mean instantly, disliked this woman. She found my it's-time-to-be-a-jerk button in less than three seconds and expertly pushed it. It had to be a record.

"Well, it's certainly not her," I remarked, hooking a thumb in Julie's direction. "And it's not him," I added, pointing down at Sherlock.

"Just answer the question," the woman snapped. "Are you Mr. Anderson?"

I was reminded of a line from a very popular sci-fi movie. If there had been a female agent in the Matrix, it would have certainly been this woman. I suppressed a smile as I imagined her ducking bullets in slo-mo.

"I am. And you are?"

"Mrs. Abigail Lawson."

My eyes narrowed and I frowned. Even though I had never met this woman before, her name wasn't unfamiliar to me. Several years ago I had spent a lot of time working on our family trees. Samantha and I, that is. This lady was on Great Aunt Bonnie's side of the tree, I was sure of it.

"Good afternoon, Mrs. Lawson," I coolly replied, refusing to stand. "What can I do for you?"

Abigail Lawson pulled out a wad of papers from her oversized purse and thrust them at me.

"You can sign these for me. Right now. Here's a pen."

I refused the pen and continued to stare at the woman, all without taking the proffered papers.

"What are these for?"

"Transfer of ownership for Lentari Cellars and the rest of my late mother's estate. It should never have been left to you. It should have gone to me. Clearly my mother wasn't in her right mind. You'd be helping me rectify that mistake by signing them. Be quick about it. I wish to leave this tiresome little town just as soon as possible."

Harry was pissed. I saw him open his mouth to say something when I cut him off.

"That won't be necessary, Mrs. Lawson. I plan on keeping the winery and the estate. Thank you so much for your more than generous offer."

"I wasn't offering to buy it," Abigail snapped, still holding the papers out to me. "You're going to do the right thing and sign everything over to its rightful owners. That's me, now sign it."

That's it. Patience just flew right out the window. In fact, I'm pretty sure it just crashed through the window in order to get away from me as fast as it could.

"The estate, and everything on it, was left to me and my wife." I slowly stood, prompting Harry and Julie to do the same. Sherlock woofed another warning. I was also pleased to see Abigail take a step back. After all, I was six feet tall and she was barely five feet four inches, even with her heels. Plus, I had to have a good hundred pounds on her. Well, let's make that seventy-five. "That makes me the rightful heir. With that being said, I am going to honor my late wife by keeping the inheritance. Her inheritance. I feel that it would be important to her. Do you get that, Mrs. Lawson? Does that compute? I don't know why your mother left everything to Samantha and me, but she did. My wife is gone, lady. For some reason fate led me here. I'm not going anywhere."

Abigail's eyes shot daggers at me. The papers she was holding were forcibly rammed back into her purse and she stormed off. I glanced down at Sherlock and patted his head affectionately.

"Good boy. I was about ready to sic you on her."

Sherlock wagged the stump of his tail and looked

back in the direction where Abigail had stormed off. The corgi turned to me and settled back to the ground, content to keep me in his sights. Harry whistled.

"That was intense. Do you know her?"

"I've heard of her, only through the family tree I worked on for Samantha's side, but I have never met her before. I'm sorry you guys had to see that."

Julie patted my shoulder.

"Don't be. She was a bitch. Anyone could see that. You know what? I think we all could use a margarita."

I laughed. I hadn't realized how much I missed being in the company of friends. Ever since Samantha's death I…

Whoops. Veered again.

"Don't you two have to go back to work?" I asked my new friends, grateful that I had someone to talk to here in town.

Julie nodded. "You're right. It probably wouldn't be good for my career if I showed back up at the station with a buzz."

Harry clapped a hand on my other shoulder.

"Tell you what, pal. Once Julie and I are done why don't we pick up a pizza and head over to your place? We can help you unpack and show you around. Julie and I have been out to the estate a couple of times and probably know it better than you."

I sat back in my chair and smiled.

"You know what, guys? That sounds like a plan. I apprecia—"

"Mr. Zack Anderson?" a gruff male voice interrupted from behind me.

I watched Harry stiffen with surprise. Julie gave a

little gasp and clutched her husband's hand. I groaned. Now what? Had Abigail returned with reinforcements?

"Yes?" I asked, turning around.

Two uniformed policemen were standing on the other side of the terrace wall, staring straight at me. Great. That nasty hag must have made a beeline straight for the cops.

"We need you to come with us."

"Is this about that lady?" I scowled and rose to my feet. Sherlock started growling. "Look, I might have lost my cool there for a bit, but there was no harm done. Sherlock, easy. They're just asking questions."

One of the cops pulled out a small notebook and made a few notes.

"So you're saying the two of you had an altercation? Were there any witnesses?"

Julie rose from her position next to Harry and approached the two officers.

"Dave. Mike. Would either of you care to tell me what's going on?"

Both officers gave a visible start as they recognized Julie.

"Jules," one of them acknowledged. "We didn't notice you there. Do you know Mr. Anderson?"

"He's a friend. He and my husband went to school together. What's going on?"

"We need to take Mr. Anderson downtown. We have some questions for him."

"Questions about what?" I wanted to know.

"Questions about the murder of Ms. Jacobs. You claim the two of you had an altercation. We'd like to get everything on record, if you don't mind."

My mouth fell open as I gawped like a love-struck teenager.

"Excuse me? I've never met her. I was referring to Abigail Lawson. You know, the grumpy old crone that was just standing here?"

The policeman with the notebook made another few notes.

"So you're saying that you physically assaulted another woman?"

"I did no such thing!" I protested. "I never assaulted anyone!"

This definitely wasn't going well. Being new to town I kinda figured the cops would be calling on me at some point to ask about the poor woman who was killed. They always seem to point the finger at the new guy. I just never imagined that they'd be incompetent. I was certain Ms. Lawson, the grumpy old hag, had somehow convinced those two policemen I was guilty of some heinous crime. Speaking of which…

"Are you accusing me of a crime?"

"That remains to be seen," the other officer said, breaking his silence. "There are things that must be explained. Take it easy. You're not being charged with a crime. Not yet, anyway. Now, would you please come with us?"

Could this day get any worse? I looked down at Sherlock, who chose that time to look up at me.

"Look, I just adopted a dog. Can I at least take him home first?"

"Do you have someone there to watch over him?" Harry asked, concerned. "You don't want to leave a new dog alone in a house by himself. Trust me. I could take him back to his kennel at my office but that'd break his heart. I can't do that to the poor boy."

"Just take the dog with you," Dave, the first cop, suggested. "The captain loves dogs."

I looked at my two friends.

"We're still on for tonight, right?"

Harry nodded. "I hope so, pal."

Julie squeezed my hand reassuringly.

"Everything is going to be fine. We'll see you tonight."

Everything was not going to be fine. In fact, in less than an hour I would be in a jail cell with a dozen inmates. Charged with murder.

THREE

I WAS UNCEREMONIOUSLY escorted to the same building I had been in earlier that day when I set up the utilities for my new house. Apparently, City Hall was on the southern side of the building while the Pomme Valley Police Department occupied the northern half.

I might as well have been cuffed. I had Officer Mike walking directly behind me, with one of his hands on the small of my back. I guess he thought I wouldn't make a break for it if I knew he was back there. Dave led our procession straight past the big front desk with the obligatory bored-looking cop, opened one of the three doors behind the front desk, and led me into a large, featureless room with a great big mirror on one wall.

I squinted at the large mirror, convinced I'd be able to see someone peering intently at me on the other side. I gave up and looked at the table. Three chairs. One on my side and two on the other.

"Have a seat, Mr. Anderson," Dave said. "Someone will be with you shortly."

I pulled the chair out, saw that the cushion had been partially ripped off, and promptly exchanged it for one of the other two on the flip side of the table. I glanced once at the mirror and sank down onto my chair. I crossed my legs and slouched. If they thought they were going to play some type of mind game with me in here by keeping me waiting, then they were in for a rude awakening. Unlike some, solitude was never something that bothered me. I've waited for over an hour on hold with a big-name computer manufacturer just to get them to troubleshoot a $10 faulty mouse that they were obligated to fix.

Fifteen minutes later the door opened and two men entered. One had solid gray hair, was shorter than I, but probably outweighed me by a good forty pounds. He was wearing a blue suit with a police badge prominently displayed where most people would put a handkerchief. The second man was younger, about my age I'd guess. He was wearing a brown suit that also had a badge hooked to his pocket. Brown Suit was carrying a cardboard box with a file sitting in plain sight on top of the box.

"What's this all about?" I demanded, as soon as the two men had taken their seats. "Would either of you care to clue me in?"

The box was placed on the table and the file was placed to the side. The younger man opened the file he had brought in with him and made a point of reading some notes on the first page. The older man looked down at Sherlock and smiled. He had to be the captain. He held his hand out and waited for Sherlock to wander over to give it a cursory sniff.

"Good afternoon, Mr. Anderson," the younger man said. The tone of his voice suggested his afternoon had been anything but good. "My name is Detective Vance Samuelson. This is Captain Jason Nelson. Thank you for agreeing to meet with us."

"Like I had a choice," I responded, folding my arms across my chest and leaning back in my chair. "You people have a helluva way to welcome new residents to this city."

Detective Samuelson tapped the folder again and nodded.

"That's right. We see here that you just moved to town. How are you finding things so far?"

I made a point of deliberately glancing around the unremarkable room I was in. I looked over at the huge one-way glass mirror on the wall I was facing.

"Rather shitty, thanks for asking. How's your day going for you?"

Samuelson looked up from the file.

"You're not having a good day, Mr. Anderson?"

I silently studied the detective for a few moments, trying to get a feel for the man. Was he trying to show me he had a sense of humor? Was it sarcasm? I turned to the captain.

"Can you tell me why I'm here? Am I being charged with a crime?"

The captain, who had been petting Sherlock, finally looked up at me. His smile melted into a frown.

"Are you familiar with 4th Street Gallery?"

"Not really. Remember the part about me just moving to town?"

"Mm-hmm. Answer the question, please."

"I've heard of it. I know I drove past it, but I've never been in it."

"Mm-hmm. Have you ever met Ms. Zora Lumen?" the captain continued.

Detective Samuelson was scribbling notes like crazy. "No."

"What about her assistant, Ms. Debra Jacobs?" Samuelson asked, looking up briefly at me as he spoke.

"No."

"Have you heard of Emelie Vång?" the detective continued.

I nodded. "Most people with access to the internet have."

"What about *Bengál*?" Samuelson prompted.

"Not until earlier today," I admitted. I immediately saw both the captain and the detective share a look. I decided I should offer a better explanation or else I was going to find myself with new living arrangements for the next twenty years or so. "I had heard of her work, but have never seen any in person. I had no idea that tiger thing was here in town. I noticed the crime scene tape on the purple door so I asked someone about it earlier. That's when he told me about what had happened and what had been stolen. He showed me a pic of it on his cell phone."

"You said you just moved to town today, correct?" Samuelson asked, checking his notes.

"Right."

"Do you make friends easily?" the captain asked. His face was impassive, neither smiling nor frowning.

"Yeah, sure. What's that got to do with anything?"

I watched Detective Samuelson scribble more notes on his notepad. After a few seconds of silence, I fidgeted in my chair.

"Do you want to know what I ordered at the coffee shop? How about where I went after I finished my bagel? How about a complete list of every place I've been today, would that help?"

Samuelson looked up and nodded.

"Actually, it would."

"Not until you start sharing some info with me, pal,"

I insisted. "I've been answering your questions. Willingly. Now it's time for me to ask a few. What's happened? What have you found that made you bring me in? I can assure you that I have nothing to do with whatever happened at that gallery."

Detective Samuelson looked at the captain for his approval. Captain Nelson gave a slight nod of his head. Samuelson removed the lid of the box and reached inside, removing something encased in a heavy clear plastic bag. The word "evidence" was clearly visible across the front of it. He studied the item for a few moments before handing it to me.

"What do you make of this?" the detective asked.

I looked at the thing in the bag. There was no mistaking what it was.

"Looks like a gun."

"That is a model 627 Smith & Wesson .357 Magnum Special," Detective Samuelson informed me. "It can hold eight bullets. Would you be surprised to learn that only seven are presently in the chamber? It has been fired once."

"That is our murder weapon," Captain Nelson smugly announced.

They were baiting me. I wasn't gonna fall for it.

"Good for you. I'm glad you found it. What does this have to do with me?"

"You're telling us you've never seen this gun before?" Detective Samuelson demanded, growing agitated.

I looked the detective straight in his eyes and didn't flinch.

"I've never seen it before in my life. Why do you ask?"

"Would it surprise you to learn it was registered to a Mrs. Bonnie Davies?" the captain nonchalantly asked me.

My eyebrows shot up. Aunt Bonnie had a gun?

"It would. This is the first I've heard of it. I really didn't know anything about her."

"You inherited all her things, isn't that right?" the detective asked, consulting another page inside the file. "You do realize that anything Ms. Davies owned now belongs to you, don't you?"

Speechless, I glanced down at the gun in my hands. They were trying to pin this on me! Don't they have ways to find out if I fired this thing? What was it, something about residue? I smiled. All those episodes of *C.S.I.* finally paid off. I looked back at the captain and held out my hands.

"If you think I fired that thing, when I didn't even know my wife's great aunt had it, then test me. Run one of those GSR tests. Or I can save you some time and simply tell you what you won't find any on my hands. Gunshot residue, that is. That'll prove to you I didn't fire that thing. Not only that, you won't find my prints on it, either."

"Don't you worry about the GSR test," Detective Samuelson assured me. "We'll be conducting that next. Do you have any idea where we found this gun?"

"I have spent less than an hour in my newly inherited house since I've moved here. I haven't a clue, pal."

"In your home."

"What? When were you in my home?"

"Earlier today."

Captain Nelson held out a hand for the file. Once the detective had passed it over, the captain slid a sheet out and showed it to me. There it was, in black and white. A search warrant. And it even had my name on it.

"Can I ask you where you found it?"

Detective Samuelson flashed a smug smile at me.

"You can ask but I don't have to answer."

"What about time of death?" I exclaimed, growing panicky. Sherlock decided he didn't like either of the two strangers and began growling at them. "When did that poor lady die at the gallery?"

"We won't know until an autopsy is done, but our Medical Examiner says it was between 10 p.m. and 2 a.m. last night."

My smile returned. Thankfully the captain noticed and instantly frowned.

"Do you want to know what I was doing at that time last night?" Naturally, there was no answer but I kept on going anyway. "Good, I'm glad you asked. I was sound asleep. At a hotel. In Ashland. I have the receipt for the room back in my Jeep. Why don't you give them a call? They can back me up."

Captain Nelson angrily reached into the box to pull out Exhibit B. This time it was a much smaller plastic bag. I could see some type of green substance in it. The bag was passed to me.

"What is this?" I asked, genuinely puzzled.

"That is a broken wine seal," the detective answered, waiting to see how I was going to react to this damning piece of evidence.

The problem was, I didn't know what I was looking at. It looked like broken pieces of plastic. This was a wine seal? Wines have seals?

"Don't play dumb with me," the captain angrily insisted. "That's the seal of Lentari Cellars. You can see the griffin right there."

"Man, I didn't even know what the winery was called until earlier today," I told the two cops. "I heard from two different people that the winery made some great wine. That would suggest that lots of people drink it, so anyone could have dropped that, dontcha think?"

Another plastic bag was produced. This one was large, even larger than the first bag. It had a collection of pamphlets, flyers, and even a hefty hardcover book in it. I caught sight of a familiar name: Emelie Vång.

"We found this in your house," Detective Samuelson proudly announced. "Explain that."

I looked at the materials in the bag. All of them were about the "sensational Swedish phenomenon" and her wonderful pieces of glass. I looked up at the detective.

"I would say that Aunt Bonnie was a fan. Come on, guys. This is all circumstantial. You're grasping at straws. I'm not the one you're looking for."

"Oh, don't worry," the captain assured me. "We saved the best for last."

I sighed loudly. Sherlock perked up his ears and stared at me.

"Fine. You have something else. Hit me with your best shot."

The final evidence baggie was produced. It contained a small spiral bound notebook with a dark blue cover.

"We found this buried in your desk," Detective Samuelson gravely said. "If you didn't kill Ms. Jacobs then you clearly know who did. And you know who took the tiger. You will start cooperating and you will start now."

I looked at the notebook with skepticism written all over my face.

"You found a notebook. Big whoop. What's that got to do with me?"

"Why don't you open it and find out?" Captain Nelson suggested.

I slid the evidence baggie with the notebook over to me, unsealed the bag, and tipped it upside down, careful not to physically touch it. I then liberated the pen Detective Samuelson was using to flip open the notebook. My heart missed a beat, and my stomach sank, as I saw what was within. I swallowed nervously.

In handwriting that looked a lot like mine were notes. Notes about the gallery, about the gallery's security, about back alleyways. There were notes about time-tables, equipment lists—ropes, pulleys, night-vision goggles, etc.—and notes about the tiger itself. It was like a burglar's shopping list.

I cursed silently. It looked as though I had researched how much the tiger was worth, where I might be able to go in order to sell it, and possible places to hide it.

"This isn't mine," I promised, looking up. "This may look like my handwriting, but it isn't. Get an expert in here. You'll see. I've never seen this before in my life."

"Suddenly you're a lot more cooperative," Captain Nelson observed.

"Only because you people think I did this. I didn't kill Debra Jacobs. I didn't steal that tiger thing. For heaven's sake, I just moved here!"

"You can drop the pretense," the captain snapped. "We found your prints on that book."

"What?! How?" I demanded. "I've never seen this book before. I've never touched it. I'm being set up!"

"I should also inform you that we are going through your phone and bank records right now," Detective

Samuelson said. "Are you sure you don't want to come clean before we find what we're looking for?"

"I have nothing to hide," I told the two cops. "You can look as long as you want. You're not going to find a thing on me. Why? BECAUSE I DIDN'T DO IT!!" I shouted. "Run your tests. Do a background check on me. You're the ones who will be apologizing to me once all of this is said and done."

There was a knock at the door.

"Enter," the captain barked.

The door opened, admitting a skinny young guy in his late teens. He ventured into the room only far enough to be within arm's reach of the captain. The teenager held out a bundle of papers and waited for Captain Nelson to take them.

"Thank you, Thomas."

Captain Nelson skimmed the pages, grunted once, and then wordlessly handed them to Detective Samuelson. As one, both cops turned to stare at me.

"What?" I asked, growing even more nervous than I already was. "What do you have there?"

The captain held up the first bundle of papers.

"This is a copy of your bank statements, going back three months. Would you care to explain why there are not one, or two, but three large deposits into your bank account?"

Say what? Three large deposits into my account? Oh. Duh. I know what he's looking at.

"Insurance payoffs," I told the captain. "My wife died in a car accident. Between our own personal insurance and my wife's employer, there were a number of life insurance policies."

"Is it usual to have more than one policy for just one person?" Captain Nelson asked, not missing a beat.

"Normally, no," I admitted. "It started with the main policy I purchased for the two of us. Then we were talked into switching to another insurance company, only I never closed out the first policy. It was such a trivial amount each month that I kept it going. Then my wife took a job that also offered life insurance. Trust me, no one thought anything would happen to us."

The second bundle was plopped down on the table.

"These are phone records," Samuelson explained. "We pulled records from both the land line as well as your wireless carrier. Know what we found?"

"I have no idea what went on with the house phone," I began as I picked up the phone report, "as I've only used it once earlier today to answer a call from my friend. As for my cell, it's going to show some activity, sure. However, unfortunately for you, you'll see that I haven't called any local numbers at all."

"Your cell phone doesn't interest me," Captain Nelson exclaimed. He slid the three-page copy of my cell phone bill out of the way and instead slid the land line report over. "The house line is another matter. They don't match up, Mr. Anderson."

I nodded. "Of course they don't. They're two separate phone lines. What's your point?"

"Your cell phone showed no suspicious activity," Samuelson reported, "but your land line had several numbers in its recent history. Local numbers."

"When did Aunt Bonnie die?" I asked. "It was, like, three months ago, wasn't it?" Both cops nodded. "What calls were made and when?"

The captain consulted his notes.

"Four. Two last night and two from earlier today."

"From my house? But I didn't get in until this morning!" I protested.

"What time?" Samuelson asked.

"About 9:15 a.m. What time was the first call?"

"A call came through at 7:30 p.m. last night, from a blocked ID."

"Clearly it wasn't for me!" I sputtered. "I hadn't arrived by that time. I was still on the road!"

"So you say," the captain said. "Do you have any witnesses? Did you stop anywhere in town?"

I thought back to the events of yesterday. Had it really been less than twenty-four hours since I had arrived in town? I hadn't stopped for gas or a bite to eat. I had been driving close to twenty hours straight. I had been anxious to start my new life as quickly as possible so I kept my stops infrequent. However, I ran out of steam around Ashland and stopped for the night.

I shook my head. "Aside from the hotel in Ashland, no. But all you have to do is pull the GPS from my phone. You'll see that I was nowhere close to the house at that time."

"So if you didn't murder Ms. Jacobs, then who did?" Detective Samuelson snapped. "Obviously someone did. I personally think that someone is you! Either that or you're involved with the person who did murder Ms. Jacobs. What do you think, captain? Do we have enough to book him?"

Captain Nelson grunted once, regarded me for a few seconds, and then nodded. He rose from the table and left without a word. Two uniformed officers appeared in the door.

"Zachary Anderson, you are under arrest for the murder of Ms. Debra Jacobs."

The two officers arrived at my side, bodily lifted me from my chair, and turned me around. Sherlock growled as menacingly as he could, but coming from a corgi, it wasn't that threatening. Cuffs were slapped on my wrists while Detective Samuelson began his spiel.

"You have the right to remain silent and refuse to answer any questions. If you give up that right then anything you say can be used against you in a court of law. You have the right to have an attorney present. If you can't afford an attorney then one can be appointed…"

I stared down at Sherlock, who again chose that time to look up at me. His head cocked to the side. I was pretty sure the little corgi was ready to bite a few ankles on my behalf, but I certainly didn't want anything to happen to him because of me.

"What's going to happen to Sherlock?" I asked as the detective finished reading me my rights.

"Who would you like to call to come get him?" Detective Samuelson asked.

"Let me guess. That'd be my one and only phone call, wouldn't it?"

Samuelson gave me a smug smile, but didn't say anything.

"I'll keep him with me. And I'd like to make my phone call, please."

I had just thought of who I was going to call. For the first time in what felt like a long time, I smiled.

"SHERIDAN RESIDENCE, this is Molly. How can I help you?"

I hesitated. The voice sounded young, maybe early

teens. I hoped I didn't have to explain who I was or why I was calling.

"Hello there. I'm hoping to speak to Mary Sheridan. Is she available?"

"She's out back. Just a second, please."

I heard the clunk as the phone was set down. Then I heard a sliding door open and a shout that was easily heard without my having to hold the phone up to my ear.

"Mom! You have a phone call!"

Several seconds of silence passed.

"I don't know. You'll have to ask. Just hurry. I'm expecting a call!"

I suppressed a smile.

An older female voice appeared on the line.

"Hello? Who is this?"

"Mary? Hello. This is Zachary Anderson."

"Who?"

"Zachary Anderson. The author. We met in person in Dallas last year at the only book signing I have ever done. It was for an alien sci-fi thriller I had released, but it didn't do that well. I admitted to you I typically wrote in, uh, another genre. Do you remember me now?"

"Oh! Mr. Anderson! How good of you to call! I didn't realize you kept my number!"

"I'm sorry. I hope you don't think it was creepy of me to do so, but whenever I come across someone that has a unique set of skills I might find useful, then I will keep their contact info handy."

"My unique skills? What do I…wait. Do you have need of a lawyer?"

I sighed heavily.

"Yes, I do. I'm in a pickle, Mary. I could definitely use some legal advice."

"What's going on?"

"I've been arrested, charged with murder."

"What?! Did you…you know…are you guilty?"

"Absolutely not!"

"And you used your only phone call to call me? How sweet!"

Holy crap on a cracker. She couldn't possibly be flirting with me, could she?

"Mary, focus. Can you help me?"

"Tell me you want to hire me. For the record."

I took a deep breath.

"Mary, I'd like to officially retain your services as a lawyer."

"Excellent. I am on the case. Would you please put the closest police officer on the phone?"

"I'd love to." I smiled as I looked over at Detective Samuelson. I handed him the phone. "She'd like to talk to you."

Understandably, trying to get someone sprung from jail isn't a quick process. All in all, it took over six hours for Mary to work her magic. I don't know how she did it, and I don't want to know. All I can tell you is that every cop I encountered on my way out of the police station was scowling at me. No doubt I've been assigned a police "tail" until this matter has been resolved. No one liked being called "inept" in any line of work. Even though I hadn't been privy to what Mary had said to the cops, I'm sure it wasn't good.

Mary had even told me that she was willing to waive her fee as long as I based a character on her in my next book. Ordinarily I tend to avoid creating characters based on real life people, so I was slow to agree to Mary's request. However, all it took for me to agree was to hear what her fee was to handle this case for me: $25,000. Did you catch that? Twenty-five grand just to make sure my sorry ass stayed out of jail. So yeah, a little show of thanks was in order for Mary's good deed.

I collected my personables, as the deputy behind the desk had called them, and walked my dog out of the police station with my head held high. Sherlock promptly pulled me to the closest tree and did his business. Thankfully, I didn't need to find a baggie.

Also, as luck would have it, City Hall was on the same side of town as the parking lot where my Jeep was. Ten minutes later Sherlock had his head out the passenger window, spraying doggie saliva all over the glass. I didn't mind. I was so glad to get out of jail that I probably could have sideswiped a tree with the Jeep and not cared.

Well, maybe a little.

I looked over at the newest member of my family. Sherlock had grown bored of the open window and had curled up on the seat. He was sitting in such a way that he was able to watch me without lifting his head.

I reached over to give him a scratch behind his ears. The corgi's tongue flopped out of his mouth and he panted contentedly. Dogs. I don't know if I can do this. I'm not set up to care for a dog. I don't have any dog food at home. For that matter, I don't have any human food, either. I never found the grocery store today, let alone did any shopping.

It was evening, and the sun was about to set. The clock on my dash said it was almost seven. I certainly hoped the offer of a free pizza dinner was still open. A quick call to Harry confirmed that it was.

"How on earth did you ever get out?" Harry wanted

to know. "Julie made some discreet inquiries and found out that you're the owner of the murder weapon, they have your prints on a notebook outlining the theft of that glass tiger, and that you couldn't explain any of it."

"I'll tell you all about it when you come over. Uh, you and Julie can still come, right? I haven't eaten anything yet and I'm pretty sure there isn't any food in the house. If there is, I wouldn't touch it with a ten foot pole."

"You bet, pal. We have the neighbor's daughter watch the kids all the time. As soon as she gets over here, we'll pick up the pizza and head over."

"One other request, Harry."

"Absolutely. What do you need?"

"Dog food. Poor Sherlock has got to be hungry. He hasn't eaten anything, either, and I know there's nothing at the house for him."

"I already have a complimentary bag of food in the van," Harry assured me. "They'll be no canine mutinies tonight."

Fifteen minutes later I pulled into the drive of my new home. As I parked in front of the detached three-car garage, I yet again felt the familiar pang of loss deep within my chest. Samantha. She would have loved this house. She's always had an affinity for houses with front porches. This one certainly fit the bill.

She and I used to…

I angrily shook my head. Sam was gone. There's nothing I could do about that. I had to live in the present, not the past. I had to take care of myself.

Sherlock gave a small yip, drawing my attention. He was staring up at me with an expectant look.

"Are you a mind reader now, sport? Don't worry. I'll

take care of you, too. I may not know what I'm doing, but I'll give it my best effort, okay?"

Sherlock seemed satisfied with that and pulled on his leash, eager to explore his new surroundings.

The best way to describe Great Aunt Bonnie's house would be to call it a country farmhouse. As I previously mentioned, the house had a large wrap-around front porch. The house wasn't huge, not by today's standards, but for a single person the 3,100 square feet, spread across two floors, was more than enough.

As I walked up the steps to the front door, I paused. I retraced my steps and looked back at the house. There, under the ground level first floor was a clear separation of building materials. There was a gradual slope near the western side of the house, revealing what I thought was a brick foundation. However, upon closer examination, I could see several narrow windows peeking out from the overgrown shrubs bordering the house.

This house had a basement! Cool! I wonder what I'd find in there. As long as it wasn't Aunt Bonnie, then I'd be fine. Harry was right. I really didn't have any idea what the house contained.

What I knew about the house was what I had picked up from the attorney who had handled Aunt Bonnie's estate. The main floor was larger than the second. There were four total bedrooms, with the master bedroom on the ground floor and three bedrooms up on the second story. The house had two full bathrooms, one on each floor, and a smaller half bathroom right off the kitchen, which is an odd place to locate a toilet, if you ask me.

Whatever. I didn't pay for it.

Sherlock and I entered through the front door. I immediately stooped down to unclip his leash. The inquisitive corgi turned to look up at me with an incredulous look on his furry face. Apparently, he couldn't believe I was turning him loose inside a strange house.

"This is your house, too, pal. Might as well become familiar with it."

Sherlock instantly veered right and began sniffing along the ground. I followed from a discreet distance. After all, I really hadn't had a chance to explore the house and didn't want him getting into anything he shouldn't.

We hit the formal dining room first. There was a large, dusty oak table with six chairs placed around it. The cushions were orange, the same shade of orange shag carpeting you've probably seen before in an elderly relative's house when you were growing up. It wasn't a pretty color. Wonder if I could reupholster those?

The dining room opened into the main family room, which could easily become my favorite room in the house. It stretched up to the second floor and had vaulted ceilings that were close to twenty-five feet high. It was huge. Too bad it had severely outdated furniture. An old blue and white couch patterned with a floral print was set in front of an honest-to-goodness wood fireplace. There was something else I hadn't noticed before: no televisions anywhere.

I vowed to rectify that deficiency the very next day, even if it meant I had to drive to nearby Medford, which was over twenty miles away. Sherlock jumped up on the couch, sniffed once at a cushion, and immediately jumped down.

I nodded and added one couch to the list.

Sherlock wandered back to the dining room and then turned left, emerging into the kitchen. This room wasn't nearly as outdated. I could tell someone had done some remodeling in here within the last five years or so. A couple of appliances could stand to be replaced, but as long as they worked, they would do for now.

The kitchen had a small island, which is where the sink was located. It was a white ceramic double sink, complete with a garbage disposal. A flick of the switch confirmed it worked, only it didn't sound too healthy to me. Sherlock barked once, not in surprise but with an annoyed edge. He hadn't barked at the disposal, but at me.

The little snot had an attitude. I slowly grinned. Good. I like that in a dog.

Continuing with his inspection, Sherlock moved into the…you know, I don't know what to call it. It's a small sitting area off of the kitchen where another dining table had been set up. This table wasn't as nice as the other, so I'll call this a breakfast nook and the other room can be the formal dining room.

Samantha would be rolling with laughter if she could see me struggling to come up with the proper names for these individual rooms. She knew full well I couldn't care less about this type of stuff.

My thoughts trailed off as Sherlock approached a closed door in the kitchen and growled. The hairs on the back of my neck stood straight up. My eyes had widened to the size of saucers and I desperately glanced around the kitchen for something to use as a weapon.

"What do you smell, boy?" I quietly asked the dog.

Sherlock growled and refused to move. Uh, oh. Was there someone else in this house besides the two of us? Hadn't the detective said that several calls were made from here while I was away? I added "change the locks" to my list of things to accomplish tomorrow.

I caught sight of a knife block on the counter. I grabbed the biggest handle I could see and pulled the knife out of the block. It was an eight-inch cleaver. What Aunt Bonnie was doing with a knife like this was beyond me but right now, I didn't argue. I was about to go Psycho on someone. I gripped the doorknob and looked over at Sherlock, who still hadn't moved and hadn't stopped growling.

"Are you ready?"

Apparently, are you ready was corgi-speak for lose your freakin' mind. He began barking like crazy and bouncing up and down, but only on his front two legs. He'd inch forward, bark like mad at the door, and then his sense of self-preservation would kick in and he'd run to the other side of the kitchen island.

"Thanks, pal," I grumbled, as I steeled myself to open the door. "All I ask is if there's a person in there, bite him any place you can reach. Okay?"

Sherlock's look of derision had me laughing. I yanked open the door, brandishing my meat cleaver, and prepared for the worst. Nothing. It was a utility room. A surprisingly new front-load, high efficiency washer and dryer met my gaze.

I turned, fully intent on scolding Sherlock, when I noticed he was still growling. Confused, I looked back in the room. What was he growling at? I spotted a laundry basket on the ground with a few pieces of clothing still in it.

"That? Do you smell the clothes? They're Aunt Bonnie's. At least I hope they are."

A thought occurred to me. What if they weren't?

Could they belong to whomever was in here earlier today? If so, what kind of stupid dumbass would take off a shirt, or jacket, and leave it in the laundry basket?

I saw a broom leaning up against the dryer and used its handle to poke the basket. Now, before I describe what happened next, it's imperative you understand my frame of mind at this point in time. I had just had one of the most stressful days of my life. I had spent a good chunk of the day in jail. I was angry, hungry, and tired, and clearly not thinking straight.

Remember that.

Something small, gray, and furry leapt out of the basket and streaked across the ground. I'm ashamed to say that I screamed like a little girl, jumped up on the dryer, and began swinging the broom through the air much like Conan wielding his broadsword. Sherlock barked once, signaling he was in pursuit.

Of course, it was a mouse. Look, I'm a dude. I'm not afraid of mice, but when you're not expecting anything to come leaping out at you, the sight of something unknown coming straight at you would be enough to send chills down the spine of even the bravest of souls. At least no one but Sherlock had seen me losing my cool over a tiny rodent.

"Have we caught you at a bad time?" Harry's voice asked from the kitchen doorway. His right hand was wrapped around a large bag of dog food slung over his right shoulder while a six pack of beer was in the other. From the way he was grinning at me I could tell he had witnessed the whole thing.

I hastily jumped down from the dryer and tried to reclaim my shattered dignity. Or what was left of it.

"When you tell this story, and I know you will, try to remember that I had a really bad day today."

"What's going on?" Julie asked as she came in the door. She was carrying a bag of groceries and a gallon of milk. She brushed by me and began putting things away in the kitchen.

"Oh, nothing," Harry called back to her, a smile forming on his face. "Zack was just showing me how high he can jump."

"Bite me, dude."

Julie looked quizzically at me and then at her husband. She shrugged and headed toward the kitchen. She plopped everything down on the counters and began unloading her bags. Bread, milk, peanut butter, Milk Bones, and several other essentials were laid out for all to see.

"Thanks, guys. I really appreciate what you're doing for me. Do you, er, know where everything goes, Julie?"

"Do you?" Julie countered as she slid the milk in the fridge. Thankfully the old Maytag was running, cold, and completely empty.

"No," I admitted.

"Then you should have no worries. Where would you like the bread?"

I got the distinct impression that she was mothering me, as though I didn't know how to care for myself. Then I realized that for all intents and purposes, I was standing in a stranger's house with no idea where anything was.

"I got you some laundry detergent," Julie added. "Something tells me you'll want to wash everything before you use them."

"Before I use what?" I wanted to know.

"Sheets, towels, linens, etc."

I looked at Harry.

"She thought of everything."

Julie pulled two large bowls she had just found from a cupboard in the kitchen island and filled one with water. Harry filled the other with dog food and both were set down on the floor for Sherlock.

Once the corgi was busy crunching through his kibble, we all took seats at the breakfast nook. The pizza was fantastic. They had brought two pizzas. I don't know where they got them, nor did I care. At least there was a pizza joint in town and that's all that mattered. As for the pizza itself, one was a meat lover's and the other was a Hawaiian.

We talked for hours sitting at that table. I recounted everything that had happened to me today, starting with meeting the attorney at the front door and ending with my triumphant release from jail. The only part I left out were the specifics of my profession. Harry had already caught me screaming like a girl. I didn't want him to know that I let people think I was one when it came to writing books.

Harry, in turn, told me about his life and how he had ended up in PV and what it had taken in order to break him out of the reckless behavior he was known for. Turns out it was a car accident. A bad one. It had almost killed him and that, apparently, was enough of a reality check to break him of his bad habits. He and Julie rekindled their romance, she talked him into going to school, and the rest is history.

We sat in those wood chairs for so long that my butt fell asleep and my legs were only moments away from going completely dead on me. Thankfully that was when Sherlock decided he needed to go outside, presumably to do his business, and barked twice by the door.

Once he was back inside, it was decided we should call it a night. They, of course, had kids who needed to go to school tomorrow. I, on the other hand, could sleep in and was really looking forward to doing just that.

Only as they were driving away did I realize they never did get a chance to show me around the property. It didn't matter. I had already spent one full day in Pomme Valley without poking around the house I had inherited. Whatever this house had to show me, it could wait until morning.

Boy, was I wrong. More on that later.

I found the master bedroom on the other side of the house. It had a huge bathroom attached to it that had dual sinks, a large walk-in closet, and a Whirlpool tub. I was also surprised to see a second porch easily accessible from a sliding glass patio door on the same wall as the bathroom.

I was about ready to turn down the bed for the night when I remembered that a little old lady used to live here. Had the sheets been changed since she had died? I decided I didn't care if they had been or not. I needed to find a fresh set.

Half an hour later, sheer exhaustion was threatening to settle in. The sheets were changed, the linens having been dumped in the utility room, and I had located a couple of boxes of my clothes. I shut off all the lights and headed to bed when I saw that Sherlock was already waiting for me. He had jumped up on the bed, claimed the left side, and was curled up by the pillows.

As soon as my head hit the pillow the dog rolled to his feet, timidly approached me, and licked my hand once.

"What was that for, Sherlock?"

The corgi nuzzled my shoulder, turned in place three times, and finally settled in right next to me. The next thing I knew both of us were out cold.

Fast forward six hours later.

I knew it was early. The sun wasn't up and it was incredibly dark in the house. The first thing I noticed was the complete absence of noise. I had lived my whole life in the city where there was always something happening. Passing trains, honking horns, helicopters flying overhead, anything and everything usually found in the city had been my white noise.

Now, in the middle of the country with my nearest neighbor a half mile away, it was quiet. Freaky quiet. Wow. I was going to have to do something about that. Maybe I could buy a white noise tape and have it…

A soft snuffling sounded nearby, causing my blood to freeze in my veins. What the hell was that? I know it wasn't me. Was there someone else in the house?

I reached for my phone. Whoever designed my smartphone included the ability to turn on the LED flash and keep it on, thus turning the sophisticated device into an unsophisticated flashlight.

My arm swept the bed and instantly found a furry body snuggled up against my right side. Memories from yesterday flooded back to me. That's right. I owned a dog now. Sherlock, it would seem, enjoyed sleeping like I did, which was flat on my back. My hand explored his sleeping form. Yep. He had all four legs sticking straight up. I gave his belly a pat, eyed the time (it was just after 5 a.m.) and rolled back over.

Unfortunately, my mind refused to go back to sleep. It began reviewing the events of yesterday, starting with the evidence the police had against me. First up was the gun. It had belonged to Aunt Bonnie. Okay, what was a little old lady like that doing with a gun? Had she felt as though she needed it for protection?

I was told Bonnie's gun was the murder weapon. Obviously, someone knew Bonnie had the gun and had known where to find it. The police had also said that there were calls placed from the house landline. That could only mean someone had been in this house for an extended amount of time.

I wasn't concerned about the literature featuring Emelie Vång. Anyone could have had that in their house. She was a well-known artist; therefore I should be able to rule out that bag of evidence.

The notebook, on the other hand, concerned me greatly. Was it just a coincidence that the writing was a close match for my own? How had my fingerprint ended up on it? How could someone have gotten samples of my handwriting in order to learn how I write? Everything I write nowadays is on the computer. It had to be a coincidence. As for the fingerprint, well… I was going to have to think about that one.

I frowned. I really didn't believe in coincidences. Here I was, brand new to town, and I find out that someone had broken into this house, placed several phone calls, and plotted out a burglary. On top of that, we need to add one murder—using Aunt Bonnie's gun—and one pissed off police department who are now convinced I am the mastermind behind the whole thing.

Someone wanted me out of the picture. That much was clear. Whoever that was had been desperate enough to kill. Would they kill again? What else could they do to try and hurt me?

My hand continued to stroke Sherlock's belly. Sherlock. Could my dog be their next target? Could they go after him in an attempt to hurt me? I mentally vowed not to let Sherlock out of my sight. I had been a dog owner for less than twenty-four hours and here I was, surprised to learn that I had become fiercely protective of the feisty canine. I blame Harry.

I tried to close my eyes and will myself back to sleep. As soon as my eyes closed, Abigail Lawson's sour face swam into view. Ah, yes. Ms. Uber Witch. I mustn't forget about her. If ever someone had motivation to get me out of the way, it'd be her. However, it was too cut and dried. Too convenient. I find out someone is trying to set me up to take the fall for a crime I didn't commit and suddenly, presto, Ms. Bitch appears and demands I bow out of the picture.

It didn't add up. Someone wanted me out of this town and I wanted to know who. Later, once I had changed the locks, bought a respectable big screen TV, found the grocery store, unpacked my stuff, and who knows what else, Sherlock and I were going to look for some answers.

Sometimes you had to stir the pot so you could see what floated to the surface.

FOUR

ONCE IT WAS full daylight, Sherlock and I were exploring the rest of the ground floor when we were interrupted just as we were heading upstairs. My cell phone was ringing and it was from an unknown number. The area code and prefix didn't match the rest of town so I knew this person wasn't local.

"Hello?"

"Is this Mr. Zachary Anderson?"

"Yes. Who's this?"

"How are you doing today, sir?"

People who don't identify themselves when I ask them to instantly put me on high alert. It usually means they're trying to sell me something. I wasn't in the mood.

"Fine. Who are you?"

"You are the new owner of Lentari Cellars, are you not?"

"That's twice, pal," I crossly told the caller.

A couple seconds of silence passed before the voice spoke again.

"Twice what?" the male caller asked, sounding confused.

"That's twice I've asked you to identify yourself. Twice now you've steamrolled right over me to change the subject. Either identify who you are and state the nature of this call or else we're done."

Another few seconds passed.

"My apologies. I represent a party that is interested in your winery, provided you are selling."

"I am not selling. And you failed to tell me who you are. You have yourself a good day."

I promptly terminated the call and stared at the phone. Who was that? He had said he represented someone who was interested in the winery. Wouldn't that automatically put them on my list of suspects?

I had to find out who had called. I managed to open the browser app on my phone and brought up a reverse phone directory to see if I could tell who the phone number belonged to. However, all I could find out was that the owner lived in Portland.

It was definitely time to check out the winery. What was the appeal? Why did people want it? What was so special about it? Did Aunt Bonnie's wine taste that good?

I whistled for Sherlock and headed toward the door. I hadn't heard the dog approach but all of a sudden there he was, waiting to go outside with me. I eyed the leash hanging on a hook next to the door.

"Do I need to put this on you? You're not going to run away, are you?"

Sherlock gave me an exasperated look, shook his collar, and then turned to stare at the door. He seemed a little too eager for my taste. I reached for the leash and immediately heard Sherlock utter something that sounded like a cross between a grunt and a low howl.

Now I was the one cocking my head.

"What was that? Are you okay?"

Sherlock whined as he looked eagerly at the door.

"Fine. You'd better not run off, pal."

I opened the door. Sure enough, Sherlock bolted outside. I took off after the dog, but he was already around the corner of the house and out of sight.

"Sherlock! Get back here! Dammit, where'd you go?"

For a breed of dog with squat little legs, that sucker could move! I saw him, ahead of me, running straight toward the large building up on the hill.

Sherlock was heading for the winery. How had he known to go there? Had he heard me? Was a dog capable of understanding human speech? I made a mental note to Google it later.

I caught up to Sherlock in front of a set of closed double doors. The lights were off inside, so I couldn't see anything through the windows.

"It's locked, pal. Sorry."

Sherlock turned to look at me. He stared, unblinking. Nothing will quite put you on edge like having a dog look at you as though you are a complete dumbass. How the little booger knew I had the keys was beyond me.

I fished out the ring of keys and unlocked the door. Sherlock and I walked through the open door together. I automatically felt along the inside of the wall to find the light switch. Once I was able to see, I whistled with surprise.

I was standing in a small storefront. This was apparently where Aunt Bonnie sold the wine she had made at Lentari Cellars. Sherlock moved to an open display stand and sniffed at a couple of dusty bottles. I picked one up and studied it.

The bottle was made of dark green glass, had a long graceful neck, and had a label that looked like ancient parchment. The words "Lentari Cellars" were printed in an elegant script across the top. Apparently, the bottle I was holding was one of the Syrahs Woody had told me about.

I ran my finger over the dark green elliptical seal located just beneath the Lentari Cellars name. Those two cops had been right. There was a big "LC" on the seal's surface, along with an image of a griffin. One of the griffin's front forelegs was extended, as though it was preparing to take a step. I put the bottle down and headed to a large swinging door that was behind the counter, marked "Employees Only". I wasn't one, but I think being the owner justified my presence there.

There were all kind of machines back there that I knew absolutely nothing about. I could see boxes of labels, corks, and empty bottles. I saw large machines with metal pipes running between them. I saw a circular machine with grooves around the perimeter that looked as though a bottle would fit into it nicely.

I could smell a faint trace of fermented grapes in the air, which really wasn't too surprising. I didn't mind the smell at all. In fact, the smell of red wine always reminded me of Thanksgiving and turkeys cooking in the oven.

Hey, I said I don't like to drink wine, but I do like it if someone decides to cook with it. Samantha was a pro at Thanksgiving. She could...

Sorry. Veered again.

Thinking of Sam right then spurred a strong feeling of nostalgia. Of family gatherings. Of accomplishing something and being proud of it. I looked around the winery and realized something. This was Aunt Bonnie's livelihood. For all I knew, this was her dream. Samantha was part of that family. She would have loved the idea of running a private winery.

I made a decision. I wanted to continue to keep the winery running. I wanted to keep Lentari Cellars producing wine. For Aunt Bonnie. For Samantha. She would have loved all this.

Great. I guess I must have felt as though I didn't have enough on my plate at the moment and one more task shouldn't hurt anything. If I was planning on reopening the winery then I was going to need to learn how to make these machines run. Or, better yet, find someone that already knows and have them run it.

Wait.

How could Aunt Bonnie, a little old lady that had been in her eighties, run a place like this? The short answer is, she didn't. She couldn't. It would have been beyond her. She must have done the same thing I was contemplating. She must have had someone doing all the work. I just had to find out who. Perhaps she kept records of it somewhere.

Sherlock had been wandering around some of the larger machines when he suddenly stopped and barked once. Great. Another mouse? I strode forward, eager to reclaim my dignity. Even if Sherlock was the only one in attendance to witness this, I had to prove I wasn't afraid of a little rodent. If it was something else, say a rat for instance, then you were going to see a Zack-shaped hole punched into the surface of the door. Holding a corgi.

"What is it, boy?" I asked as I navigated around the large machines. I had to watch out for low lying pipes or else I would end up clotheslining myself.

I found Sherlock staring at something on the ground. I rounded a large circular tank and came to a stop. Well, it wasn't a mouse and it wasn't a rat. It was much worse.

It was a shoe.

The problem was, the shoe wasn't empty. The foot was still there. Swallowing nervously, I walked around the large tank and cursed. As much as I didn't want to find the rest of the owner of that shoe, I was secretly hoping it'd be just the shoe and the foot, as grisly as that'd be. Nope, it was all there. Or should I say "he" was there. I'd like to tell you that I was able to look at the still form that used to be a living person and check for clues, but I wasn't. I could see that it was a man wearing black jeans and a red shirt, that's it. I wasn't getting any closer.

What was I supposed to do? The movies always depicted the hero bending down to check for a pulse, maybe inspect the body to see if they could determine cause of death. Hell no. I wasn't touching that thing. Besides, the ashen complexion of the skin made checking for a pulse a moot point. I looked down at Sherlock, who was cautiously inching closer toward the dead body.

"Do you know if it's possible to be arrested twice in less than twenty-four hours?"

Thirty minutes later I had what looked like the whole town on my doorstep. Seven police cars, which I later learned constituted the entire fleet of cars the PVPD had at their disposal, two fire trucks, and two ambulances were parked outside.

Detective Samuelson was the first to arrive on the scene. I swear he sashayed into the back room of the winery, hands clasped behind his back, and smiling that arrogant smile of his.

"Good afternoon, Mr. Anderson."

I nodded once.

"Detective."

"Care to tell me what happened here?"

"It was just as I described it. My dog led me up here. I unlocked the door, came in, followed Sherlock back here and found the body. Like that."

"Do you know him?" Samuelson asked, pulling his small notebook from a concealed pocket.

"I've never seen him before."

"You say you had to unlock the door?"

"Yes," I said, nodding my head.

The detective retraced his steps back to the front door and inspected the locks. The crime scene unit arrived then and began to process the scene. Sherlock and I were ordered away from the building, which we were more than happy to oblige. Since they were more interested in asking questions than slapping cuffs on me, I decided to cooperate and bite my tongue.

Another thirty minutes passed. I saw a news van pull into my driveway. A woman wearing a bright blue business suit, with sneakers, jumped out of the passenger side of the van before it had even come to a halt. I watched her yank the sliding door open, reach in to grab a camera, and hand it to the driver as he came around the van.

I groaned. How do I keep getting myself in these situations?

I hadn't realized it, but Samuelson had approached from behind and had been watching me closely for the last couple of minutes. He nudged my shoulder to get my attention.

"You do realize you don't have to talk to them if you don't want to."

"Why are you being nice to me all of a sudden?" I asked, perplexed. "Yesterday you were convinced I had killed that lady in the gallery."

"I'm still not convinced you didn't do it, but as for the guy back there? He's been dead between twelve and twenty-four hours, according to what the M.E. just told me. No signs of trauma, no blood anywhere. It looks like he just keeled over. We won't know what killed him until an autopsy is done. Personally, I think he was killed elsewhere and dropped here, but don't tell the captain I said that."

An overwhelming sense of relief swept over me. I wasn't going to be thrown in jail again. At least, not yet.

"Is there any way you can make them leave?" I quietly asked the detective, pointing at the news van.

"This is your property, right?" Samuelson asked as we both watched the crew prepare for a shot.

"Yes."

"Then you need to tell them that this is private property and ask them to leave. If they refuse then they are criminally trespassing. Then we can get involved. Can you do that?"

"Gladly."

I strode toward the news lady, who saw me coming. She whipped out her microphone and walked purposely toward me as the cameraman lifted the large camera to his shoulder.

"Clara Springfield, Channel 11 News, Medford. Are you Zachary Anderson, owner of the winery here?"

"I am," I said as I nodded. I looked at the camera and gave it a less-than-friendly smile. "You are on private property and I'm hereby requesting, on camera, that you leave. Will you comply?"

The news reporter ignored me.

"What can you tell us about the dead body you found in the winery today?"

I turned to look back at Samuelson.

"I asked, I informed, she ignored. Will you do the honors?"

Samuelson nodded, his face becoming grim. He stepped directly in front of me and stared at the un-blinking reporter.

"The homeowner has refused to be on camera. He has asked that you leave. I'll give you five minutes to pack your gear and go."

Sherlock and I sat on the steps leading up into my house and watched the news crew argue with Detective Samuelson. They were clearly not happy about being forced to leave. I didn't care. I didn't want to compound my problems here by plastering my mug all across town. I'm sure I was already the subject of many a conver-sation throughout PV by now and I didn't want to add any more fuel to the fire.

I watched the detective. Maybe he wasn't such a prick after all. I definitely owed him a beer for scaring off the reporters.

Once the news van had departed Samuelson walked back over to me and took a seat next to me on the front steps. With a sigh, he turned to give Sherlock a friendly pat. The corgi, in turn, licked his hand in greeting. After a few moments Detective Samuelson held his hand out to me.

"I think we got off on the wrong foot. Let's try again, shall we? Vance Samuelson, detective, Pomme Val-ley PD."

I took the detective's hand.

"Zack Anderson. Writer. Oh, and winery owner. I should also mention I'm anti-wine."

"You moved to the wrong city," Samuelson observed.

"I've heard that more than once in the last two days, detective."

"Call me Vance."

"I will if you call me Zack."

Vance finally grinned.

"You don't like hearing yourself called Mr. Anderson? Let me guess. It reminds you of your father."

"No, it reminds me of Neo, from The Matrix."

Vance let out a short bark of laughter. Sherlock, concerned that he had been hurt, sidled closer and pushed his snout into the detective's chest.

"I'm alright, boy," Vance assured the corgi. "Thanks for checking. I appreciate it."

"You're talking to that dog as though he understands you."

Vance turned to me with surprise etched all over his face.

"You've never owned a dog before, have you? They are some of the most intelligent, compassionate creatures I have ever seen. Personally? I love German Shepherds. I've owned them my whole life. I'll admit there are a number of words I have to spell around my house. If I so much as pick up my keys or put on my shoes then Anubis is all over me."

I stifled a laugh. "Anubis, huh?"

"My wife minored in Egyptology," Vance offered by way of explanation.

"What does one do with an Egyptology degree?" I wanted to know.

The detective grunted once, shrugged, and shook his head.

"I have to tell you you're still a suspect," Vance informed me.

Dick. I was just starting to like the guy.

"But I also want to say that I do think you're being set up," Vance continued.

Well, there's a start.

"Uh, thanks?"

"Captain Nelson feels you are involved with this whole mess."

"I'm not," I insisted.

"The evidence suggests otherwise."

"I want to know about that notebook," I told the detective. "Is it a coincidence the writing looks like it could be mine?"

"I'd be more concerned about the fact that your prints were found on it," Vance told me, scratching behind one of Sherlock's ears. "If what you say is true, then there is definitely someone out there that wants to do you in."

"But who?" I demanded. "I don't know anyone in town."

"Didn't you say you had a friend in town earlier?" Vance asked.

"Woody? From the toy store? Well, he's more of a recent acquaintance. I met him at the café."

"And Dr. Watt?"

I stared at the detective with an incredulous look.

"How could you possibly know that?"

Vance returned the stare with a "you've got to be kidding" look on his face.

"Who were you having lunch with yesterday?"

Okay, they had me there.

"Alright, I'll give you that one. How did you know he was a friend of mine?"

"Do you have lunch with that many strangers and their wives?" Vance asked with an indifferent air about him.

"Point taken. You must have had me followed. Great. So, Vance, what happens now?"

We turned to watch the fire trucks and the ambulances leave. Five of the police cars had already gone, leaving only two in front of the house. The coroner had left twenty minutes earlier.

"Now it's a waiting game. Let the crime scene boys do their thing."

Sounded tedious.

"How long will that take?"

Vance shrugged and stood up.

"As long as necessary. My guess is they'll be here for at least several more hours. I wouldn't plan on re-opening the winery until they've finished."

"I couldn't even if I wanted to."

Vance gave me a sidelong glance.

"Why not?"

"I don't know a thing about making wine. I don't know how Bonnie did it. She had to have someone helping her, but I have no idea who."

Vance pulled his little notebook back out and flipped it open.

"What are you writing in there?" I asked.

"Check into winery's previous manager."

"As a possible murder suspect?" I asked. "Why?"

"Maybe it's someone who wants the winery for himself," Vance said, stowing the notebook. "Have you had anyone ask you if the winery was for sale? Believe it or not, wineries value their recipes and will do anything to keep them a closely guarded secret."

"Enough to kill?" I asked, skeptical.

Vance nodded. "Oh, yeah. Think about it. Let's say one of the wineries around here started selling out every single time a batch was made, would that not raise an eyebrow or two? Would that not generate a negative feeling or two from the other winery owners?"

"Possibly," I admitted. "Someone did call first thing this morning and ask if the winery was for sale."

"Really? Who was it? Did they say?"

I shook my head. "No. I kept asking and they kept ignoring. So I hung up on 'em."

"Do you still have the number?"

I dug out my cell, pulled up my call history, and showed it to the detective. Vance jotted the number down in his notebook.

"I'll check into it."

"What am I missing, Vance? A winery can't be worth that much, can it?"

"What if the demand was so high that there were waiting lists before you could even get a bottle?" Vance countered.

"I'd say that'd be every winery owner's wet dream."

"Yep. That's what Lentari Cellars had going for it. Look back there. Do you see those fields? Practically everything you're looking at is part of your winery."

I looked at the dusty, dirty brown fields filled with scraggly, sickly looking grape vines. It didn't look that spectacular to me.

"Lentari Cellars hasn't produced a bottle since several months before your great aunt died. I don't know what recipe she used, nor do I know if she was even the wine master. However, I do know a lot of people would be anxious to snap up a bottle should they go on sale."

"Are you a wine aficionado, Vance?"

He nodded. "I am, but there aren't many good wines I can afford on my salary."

"Have you ever tried a bottle from Lentari Cellars?"

"Your aunt's winery made a great Syrah. It was my wife's favorite."

"Come with me."

Sherlock was already one step ahead of me. The little corgi led us to the front of the winery and trotted through the open door, as though he owned the place. I quickly scooped him up and led Vance inside. I selected a bottle of the Syrah I had noticed earlier in the day from a rack that had several bottles of each type the winery made and presented it to the detective.

"I can't take that," Vance protested. "I'm sure there's all kinds of waiting lists."

"It's my winery, my bottles, and my choice. Take it as a way of saying thanks for forcing that news crew to leave earlier."

Vance took the bottle and thanked me profusely. Sherlock and I followed him back to the house as he headed toward his car. He turned and gave me a business card.

"If Sherlock finds any other dead bodies you be sure to let me know."

Sherlock barked once, as if he were viewing it as a challenge.

"Right. You got it. Vance, let me ask you one more thing."

The detective had just stepped inside his Oldsmobile sedan when he heard the question. He cranked the window down and stared expectantly at me.

"Honestly, pal. Am I screwed? Someone is taking great pains to set me up and words cannot even begin to describe how much I don't want to go back to jail."

I could see that Vance was truly giving the question some thought. He shook his head.

"No police captain wants to have an open murder investigation in their city, let alone a small town like Pomme Valley. Captain Nelson wants this case closed as quickly as possible."

"What do you think I should be doing?" I asked.

"See if you can get me a list of anyone who would benefit from you being locked away."

"Easier said than done, but I will try to come up with something for you."

After the detective left, I checked in with the crime scene guys. They told me they'd be there at least another hour or two. The COD was still unknown, they said, but it did look like the guy was killed somewhere else and dumped there. There really wasn't much evidence to collect. I told them I was going to run some errands and that I'd be back.

"Come on, Sherlock. We've got a long list of things to do today, buddy."

Two hours later Sherlock and I were pulling away from Rupert's Gas & Auto. I had gone looking for someone that could change out my locks, but was informed this town didn't have a dedicated locksmith. Un-freakin'-real. This had to be the only town in the U.S. where the town's sole locksmith worked part-time as an auto mechanic. Thankfully he told me he'd swing by after work and redo all my locks.

I had to drive to Medford in order to find a store that sold a television larger than thirteen inches. Seriously, what was it with this town? Were people that afraid to get in touch with the outside world? I looked at the 50-

inch LED sitting in the back of my Jeep. I couldn't wait to fire that baby up.

I was cruising down Main Street, looking for the town's only grocery store, Gary's Grocery, when Sherlock jerked his head up from where he had been curled up and woofed a warning. That got my attention. What did he see? What was the saying? If my dog doesn't trust you, then I won't? I was curious. I wanted to see what had attracted Sherlock's attention. I slowed for a couple of pedestrians crossing the street and glanced up and down the rows of stores. I really didn't see anything that warranted a second look.

Sherlock woofed again. This time he stepped up onto the door's arm rest, bringing the level of his head up so he could see out the window, and barked again. The corgi was staring straight at one of the shops. In fact, it had a bright purple door that, if I wasn't mistaken, formerly had a big yellow "X" in crime scene tape blocking the way. Looked like the owner had finally taken the tape down.

"Are you looking at that?" I asked Sherlock. The corgi turned to look at me, whined once, and returned his gaze to the purple door. He barked again. "That's the gallery where all this trouble started. Why are you barking at it? There's nothing there. Calm down."

Ever try telling a dog to calm down? Has it ever worked? Probably worked as well for you as it did for me. I was ignored. Something about that store had caught the corgi's attention and he was demanding I do something about it.

"Fine, fine. We can stop by to take a look. Provided they're open and they don't mind dogs. Will that shut you up?"

Sherlock yipped excitedly. I still wasn't convinced that a dog could understand what I was saying, but that yip had certainly sounded like a "yes" to me. Besides, I strongly doubted the gallery would be open. After all, someone had lost their life in there.

There were several places to park curbside. The wine festival was clearly over, as the amount of foot traffic was much more manageable. Thankfully, the incessant rain had tapered to a light drizzle. I parked my Jeep and walked around to the passenger side as though I was opening the door for a date. Sherlock was sitting on the passenger seat, waiting patiently to be placed on the ground. I gathered the corgi in my arms and gently set him on the sidewalk.

"There you go, your royal highness. You behave yourself, you got it? No peeing, pooping, or whatever else dogs do, okay?"

We stepped up to the bright purple door and I experimentally tugged at the handle, not really expecting the gallery to be open. Much to my surprise the door swung open on well-greased hinges. Sherlock darted inside just as soon as there was enough room for him to slip through. I had a few more moments to wait.

4th Street Gallery was nothing like I expected it to be. I thought art galleries were supposed to be tasteful; immaculate. Clean. I had expected to see maybe one or two paintings on each stark white wall with a spotlight or two aimed at each one. Since the gallery obviously housed the *Bengál* at one point I was also expecting to see sparkling clear display cases with all manner of sculptures in them.

Just then my ears picked up Bon Jovi's *Slippery When Wet* coming from the back of the store. I nodded.

I was starting to like this Zora person. I had expected to hear some cheesy harp music upon setting foot inside.

I hummed along to "Livin' on a Prayer", even checking the area to see if the coast was clear to perform a little air guitar during the solo. I found Sherlock facing an empty glass display case. Was this where the tiger had been? Wrapping the leash tightly around my hand I returned my attention to what lay before me. This gallery was something else.

Imagine you had an enormous amount of inventory to showcase and you only had limited space to do it. How, then, would you display your wares? Cover every square inch of open wall space with paintings? Shelves holding sculptures? Maybe an easel or two set in the middle of the floor, containing works from the week's featured artist?

That didn't even come close to describing what I saw. One of the four walls, the one immediately on my right as I stepped through the door, was covered from floor to ceiling in paintings, like the world's best Tetris player had been hard at work making use of every square inch of space. The wall directly in front of me had a tiny office in the far-left corner. The rest of the wall was an homage to Native American art. I saw bows, arrows, and woven blankets tastefully arranged all across the wall, interspersed by old photographs of teepees, Native Americans riding on horseback, or posing for pictures.

The other two walls were what had drawn my attention the moment I stepped through the door. They had floor to ceiling shelves with one of those mobile ladders on a track that librarians used to reach books on the top shelf. Stacked on the shelves, looking remarkably like rows of books, were more paintings. My eyes widened. I hadn't ever seen that many paintings in the same place at the same time. There were so many of them that Zora had resorted to storing them like books.

I frowned. How were you supposed to sell the paintings if the customers couldn't see what you had for sale? Perhaps she was continuously rotating the paintings hanging on the wall with those that were stored on the shelves.

"Good afternoon," a soft, sultry voice announced, breaking the silence. I immediately got the impression the speaker had smoked one too many cigarettes in their day.

I turned to see who had spoken. I had been so preoccupied with taking in as much of the cluttered store as I could that I hadn't noticed anyone else. Neither had Sherlock, because he started growling the moment the figure stepped out from behind an easel holding a large bulky painting.

The person was tall and gaunt, wearing blue jeans and an oversized sweater. Gray hair was pulled back into a low ponytail and hung past his shoulders. Her shoulders. I couldn't tell if I was looking at a man or a woman. I studied the face. High cheekbones, narrow nose. Got it. Had to be a woman. This must be Zora. I should introduce myself.

"How's it goin'?" I answered, looking up from the large painting of a barn that had been concealing him from sight.

"It is 'going' well," the mysterious shopkeeper responded, using a neutral, if not patient, tone of voice.

I got the distinct impression my greeting was being mocked. The jerk.

"It's a nice place you got here."

"Quite."

Stuck up snob.

"Would you mind if I looked around?"

"No."

"Not much of a talker, are you?" I jovially asked, using the friendliest tone I could muster.

"Perhaps."

I moved right, intent on inspecting the huge Tetris wall. More specifically, I wanted to put some distance between myself and Morticia Addams. She gave me the creeps.

I whistled as I looked up at the wall crammed full of paintings. Most, if not all, were not my style. Bowls of fruit, running horses, quaint cottages, babbling brooks. Nothing that I'd be willing to hang in my new house. Then again, if I'm not mistaken, there are a few paintings on my living room wall that could have been easily purchased from this shop, so I was not one to talk.

I became aware of a presence just behind my right shoulder. Great. Morticia was following me around the store. That had to rank right up there in my top three pet peeves of all time: trying to successfully frost a cake, emptying the dishwasher, and being followed by a salesman as you looked through a store.

Picking up on the scowl that was forming on my face, Sherlock looked over at the still figure of the gallery worker and woofed a warning. I glanced down at the corgi and gave him a pat on the head. Sherlock gave Morticia a final look before pulling on his leash, leading me toward the far left of the Wall of Paintings.

The Addams family wannabe followed closely behind. I sighed once and faced my shadow.

"Hello again. Is there something you need?"

"No."

"Afraid I'll pull one of 'em off the wall and make a break for it?"

"No."

"Then why are you following me?"

"To be of service."

"What service?"

"To help you with your purchase."

"Purchase? What purchase?"

The gaunt figure smiled. Ever hear the expression "when your blood runs cold"? That's what mine just did. It was a creepy sensation. My skin broke out in goose bumps and Sherlock woofed another warning.

"You are here for a purchase. Which painting would you like?"

"Uh, I wasn't planning on buying anything, pal."

"Nonsense," the demure voice argued. "It's why you're here, is it not?"

"Truth be told, I just wanted to look around."

Sherlock pulled on his leash, leading me over to a painting with a bright orange wooden frame. It depicted a nude woman standing on her right foot. Her left foot was lifted, as though she was taking a step. She was facing away, but partially turned so that the profile of the left side of her body was visible. I had seen the style of painting before, back in high school. I liked it now just as much as I had then, which is to say, I didn't.

The painting looked sloppy; blurry. The picture had a lot of oranges and browns on the walls and on the bed, and the carpet the woman was standing on was green with orange blotches on it.

Not an attractive painting.

"Ah. After the Bath, by Edgar Degas. It was painted in 1883 and is a classic example of French Impressionism. This is only a reproduction, of course. An excellent choice."

The gallery worker had the tenacity to unhook the painting from its holder on the wall, carry it over to a nearby work table, and start to wrap it up! I wasn't buying that. Are you kidding me? It was ugly! I make fun of people who have art like that in their home. I certainly wasn't going to be one of them.

I started to protest when the top right corner of the frame caught my eye. There was a dark reddish smudge on it, as though it had been gripped by someone with paint on their fingers. A dirty, or marked, frame wasn't something you'd typically find in an art gallery.

My eyes widened. For the second time in as many minutes my blood ran cold. A dark red smudge? On the frame of a painting that just happened to be in a gallery where a murder took place the previous day? You can't tell me that it wasn't a coincidence.

"Umm, excuse me? I think you need to put that painting down."

As though it was the most normal request she had ever heard, she gently set the painting down and leaned it against the corner of the closest easel. She turned to look expectantly at me, as if waiting for an explanation. I pointed at the painting's top right corner.

"There's something on the frame. Right there. Tell me that's not blood."

The lady's smooth demeanor finally cracked. Her

eyes widened with shock and horror as she saw the blood. Aghast, she looked back at me. I sighed and pulled out my cell.

"Don't worry, I'll call 'em. I have them on speed dial."

FIVE

"WHAT IS IT with you, anyway?" Detective Samuelson demanded as he yanked open the door to the gallery. "Are you trying to see how many times your name comes up on our radar?"

I was sitting in an arm chair just inside the front door. I looked up at Vance and then promptly pointed straight down at Sherlock, who by this time had curled up by my feet.

"It's not me. It's him. I was driving by when he started barking and whining. He came straight in here and then pulled me over to that painting. Morticia there assumed I wanted to buy it."

"Morticia?" Samuelson asked, confused. He turned to see who I was pointing at. "Her name is Zora, not Morticia."

Got it. Not an Addams Family fan and no sense of humor whatsoever. I pointed at the painting, still propped up on the easel.

"Would you please check that out and tell me this is one big false alarm?"

Vance's brows furrowed as he caught sight of the dark smudge on the painting's bright orange frame. He squatted down next to the piece of art and peered intently at the mark.

"It's paint, right?" I asked hopefully.

Vance shook his head. "Looks like blood to me. Hold on. I'll check."

Vance pulled out a small gray zippered pouch from within his inside jacket pocket, extracted one of those swab things I've always seen on TV, and swiped it along the frame. Then he produced a small test tube, dumped the swab head first into the tube, and then added a couple of drops from two different bottles. The swab turned pink.

"Well, it's official, sports fans," Vance announced, with exaggerated bravado. "We have blood on the frame."

"Do you always carry around a blood tester kit thing-amajig?" I asked as I pointed at the gray case Vance had set on a nearby counter.

"What about it? It's just the Kastle-Meyer test. Swab the substance, add hydrogen peroxide, and then introduce the phenolphthalein solution. If it's blood, then the swab will turn pink. Most detectives will leave their kit in the car. I like having mine with me when I'm on duty." The detective turned to Zora, who was sitting on a nearby chair. "Ms. Lumen, is it safe to say this painting was taken from that spot on the wall over there?"

"Yes," Zora's eerily neutral voice answered.

"I hope you understand that this painting has to come with me. I have to get it to the lab so they can have the blood tested."

"It's Debbie's blood," Zora whispered. Her already gaunt face seemed even more withdrawn, more sunken. "There's no need to test it."

"Why don't you let us be the judge of that?" Vance said, as he gave the art gallery owner a guarded smile. "In fact, we'll probably have to bring a team back in here and check every painting to see if the original team missed anything else."

"Please don't," Zora moaned. "I don't think my heart could handle another surprise if anything else turned up."

Frowning, I turned to Zora.

"So you're saying you're okay if there's another bloodstain somewhere and it remains undiscovered? Would you want something like that lurking behind a painting?"

Zora fixed me with her steel gray eyes.

"You have a point, young Zachary."

What was this? She knew my name?

"Oh, yes," Zora confirmed, correctly guessing what I had been thinking. "I know who you are."

"How?" I inquired, hoping to prove to Vance that I had never met Zora before. I had already noticed he had pulled out his notebook and was taking more notes. "We've never met before today. I swear!"

"Who are you trying to convince, pal?" Vance asked, as he continued writing in his notebook.

"We have never met before today," Zora confirmed.

My respect for the creepy store owner rose a few notches. Someone was finally backing up my story.

"So, how do you know me?" I asked, as soon as Zora was looking back at me.

She slowly stood, retreated to her tiny office in the back corner, and reemerged holding a folded newspaper.

"Your picture was in the paper."

I paled. Harry never mentioned the paper had a picture of me. How did they get it? Where did they get it? Who was supplying these people with information about me?

I took the paper and unfolded it. Great. That's just great. Not only was my picture in the paper, but it had made the front page! It was a picture of me and Sam, but the photo had been cropped so that only I was visible. That picture, I knew, had been taken last year at the last family get together Samantha and I had attended.

So who was supplying the newspaper with all this information about me? Was it Abigail? The article went on to talk about my inheritance, Sam's death, and my intention to relocate from Arizona. The article was dated ten days ago. I had only made the decision to move a few weeks before that. So who was the mole?

I vowed to find out.

"Do you need me for anything else?" I asked.

Vance looked at me and then deliberately looked down at Sherlock.

"Ok, little fella. You seem to have a knack for finding things that need to be found. Is there anything else in here we need to know about?"

Sherlock gave the surroundings a passing glance before he rose to his feet and headed toward the door.

"I guess that's a 'no'," I told Vance.

Vance carried the painting outside, tried to slide the large object into the back seat of his car and, when that didn't work, popped open his trunk. He watched Sherlock and me get back into the Jeep.

"Hey, Zack. Do me a favor?"

Surprised, I glanced over at the detective who was now trying to figure out how to get the painting into his trunk without damaging it. "Sure. What do you need?"

"Stop calling me."

I laughed as I pulled away from the curb.

Sherlock and I finally found the grocery store. It

was much smaller than what I was used to. Ever been in one of those gas station convenience stores? It was about that size. I parked my Jeep in a spot next to a tree, cracked a window, and gave Sherlock a friendly pat. I told the corgi he had to stay put. Even though I knew this was a pet friendly town, I was pretty sure he wouldn't be allowed inside the store.

Sherlock patiently curled up on his seat and settled down to wait.

"Are all dogs as well-mannered as you are?" I asked as I ruffled his ears. "You are a good dog, boy."

Sherlock licked my hand as a way of saying thanks.

Half an hour later we were cutting down 5th Street, heading toward the next stop on my list, namely the post office. Sherlock, who had been snoozing in his seat, suddenly leapt to his feet and began barking. I stared quizzically at the buildings and people we were driving by. As far as I could tell there was nothing out of the ordinary. I gave the corgi a friendly pat, which seemed to mollify him, and we continued on our errands.

By the time we made it back to the house, I had managed to check off everything on my To Do list, aside from meeting with the locksmith in a few hours. I lugged my new television into the front sitting room, cleared a spot for it on the floor, plugged it in, and then...

Houston, we have a problem.

Let me pause here for a moment. Ever watch a standard definition show on a high definition television? The picture is grainy and the sound is terrible. But you know what? It's better than watching a "No Signal Detected" message bouncing around the screen. Guess I should have thought to look for a cable hookup.

A quick perusal through the phone book had me tossing it angrily across the room. Guess what else Pomme Valley doesn't have? Yup. No cable. There wasn't even anything for a set of rabbit ears to pick up. No wonder Aunt Bonnie didn't have a television in her house. There was literally nothing to watch.

Very well. Tomorrow's list had been started: contact satellite provider. I should be able to find someone who could provide service for this area. This isn't the Stone Age, for crying out loud.

My thoughts drifted back to the events inside the gallery from earlier today. A few questions had recently sprung up that were screaming for an answer. Most of them centered on my new dog. First of all, how had Sherlock known to check inside the gallery? That cute little furball had headed straight toward the only painting that had traces of blood on it. I know. Vance called me several hours later to let me know that a couple of investigators had sifted through each and every single painting in Zora's gallery and had found no additional blood. They even took the time to check all the paintings lining the floor-to-ceiling shelves on the other two walls.

No blood. Not anywhere. And not only that, the blood was only on the painting's frame. Nothing had been transferred to the wall. What did that mean? Why had Debra touched only the one painting? The entire wall had been covered in pieces of art, yet the blood had only found its way onto the one painting. Why? What had Debra been thinking? Better yet, what had she been doing? Was it even her blood?

Second, how did that little dog know to check the

winery earlier today? Coincidence? Could Sherlock have smelled the body in there?

I shuddered. Disgusting, but a distinct possibility. I knew all dogs had a highly developed sense of smell. He must have caught a whiff of the dead body. It was the only explanation I could come up with.

The photo of Samantha and me on the front page of the Pomme Valley newspaper really bugged me. Had Abigail been the person to leak it to the press? Had she angrily informed everyone that Sam and I had erroneously inherited Lentari Cellars when it should have been hers? Had she been the one who had planted my fingerprint on that notebook?

I shook my head. I still didn't have a clue how anyone could have gotten my prints in the first place. It didn't make sense. I had to be missing something. Yes, Abigail Lawson was the perfect person to pin this on. She wanted the winery and was very upset her mother had left her entire estate to someone besides her. She certainly had the motivation and hadn't had any qualms about voicing her opinions.

I started to pace in the living room. Sherlock, content to watch me from the blue and white floral sofa, watched me wear a path into the carpeting.

"Ok, pal," I said, addressing the corgi, who instantly perked up once he had noticed I was paying attention to him, "since you're so good at finding these clues, how about giving me a hand?"

Sherlock blinked twice as he stared at me.

"You found the dead body and you found the blood on the painting. If I'm ever going to be able to clear my name, then we're going to have to launch our own investigation. With the exception of Vance, the whole police department thinks I'm involved. I'm not. You know that. I know that."

Blink. Blink.

"So how do I make everyone else understand that? Where do I go from here?"

Sherlock rose to his feet and jumped down from the couch. He headed toward the kitchen, stopped, and looked back at me, as if to say, you asked for my help so try to keep up. Once he saw that I was following, he headed through the kitchen and stopped at the door leading into the utility room. I automatically reached for the broom, which was leaning up against the wall nearby.

"Is there something in there you want me to see? It had better not be that mouse again or you and I are gonna have words."

Sherlock sniffed along the bottom of the door. He looked back up at me and whined. Gripping the broom handle tightly, I opened the door. Sherlock pushed by me and inspected the room. He glanced once at the now empty laundry basket before he moved to a large, old-fashioned trash can, the kind where you have to step on a little lever on the front of the can so that the lid will pop open.

"It's a trash can. What about it?"

Sherlock barked once. He nudged the trash can with his nose. Great. I vowed to all present that if there was a mouse in there, then I wouldn't turn into a twelve-year-old girl.

I stepped on the lever. The can's lid popped up so hard that it smacked the wall behind it, giving off a loud clang. Thankfully, there wasn't anything in the can that wanted out. I could only see, well, trash.

"There's nothing there, Sherlock."

The corgi paced in front of the trash can, whining loudly. I pulled off the flip-open lid and tipped it down so he could see for himself there wasn't anything there.

"Look. Just trash. Now will you let it go?"

Sherlock stretched his neck out and took several steps forward, effectively burying his snout in the can. When I pulled the can away, I could see that there was a twisted wad of paper in the dog's mouth.

What followed was an extensive, drawn out game of tug-of-war. While trying to retrieve whatever it was that Sherlock had picked up, I learned something about dogs that day. First, dogs have a very playful personality. Sherlock absolutely loved the attention I was giving him as I chased his furry butt through the house, trying to yank the paper out of his mouth.

The second was something I had already witnessed earlier, and that was the speed with which a corgi could move. Sherlock could essentially run laps around me and make me feel like a lumbering incompetent.

The third piece of trivia I learned about dogs was that they absolutely loved to play keep-away. Sherlock, being low to the ground, could take corners at Mach 1. I, trailing hopelessly behind without a chance of catching up, had all the stealth and dexterity of an adult hippo.

Ten minutes later found me sitting on the couch in the living room, sides heaving, and completely out of breath. Sherlock padded back into the room and looked at me with concern written all over his canine features. He spit the soggy, twisted paper at my feet and promptly sat. I do believe the little bastard was worried about me. Condescending little puke.

"Don't even think you won this round. I let you win."

I picked up the damp paper and untwisted it to see what it was. My eyebrows shot up with surprise and I forgot all about the fact I was holding on to a something that was soaked with doggie drool. It was a copy of the Pomme Valley Gazette and it was dated ten days ago. Yes, it was the same issue I had seen before in Zora's art gallery. There was my picture, right on the front page, only this time I was sporting a handlebar moustache and a tiny goatee. Someone had doodled on the pic. From inside a house that was supposed to be empty.

It was definitely time to consider adding a security system to the house. I don't like knowing that someone had spent time in this house, going through whatever Aunt Bonnie left lying around. I had to assume whoever had been squatting inside this house after Aunt Bonnie's death was the same person who was doing their damnedest to set me up to take the fall for Debra Jacobs' murder.

I looked at the shredded newspaper and then over at a nearby clock. It was only 1:30 p.m. There was still time enough to do what I had in mind. I think it was high time I started to try clearing my name.

"Want to go for another ride, Sherlock?"

There's another word I'm going to have to start spelling around that dog. Wow. You'd think I just offered him the world's biggest doggie biscuit. Sherlock ran straight toward the door and then looked back at me with an exasperated expression, as if the only thing he could see was the out-of-shape lardball I felt like whenever I was around him.

We were headed north on 5th Street, approaching Main, when Sherlock began barking again. I instinctively glanced to my right to see what the little fellow was barking at. Ah. Harry's office was quickly approaching on the right. Clearly, Sherlock harbored some strong feelings about that place and was voicing his resentment. Or perhaps he was bragging to his former cellmates that he was now living the high life? I turned left onto Main Street and Sherlock promptly fell silent.

Five minutes later I was pulling into the offices of *Pomme Valley Gazette.* I wanted to speak with the reporter who had written the feature about me and find out who had given him his information. How had the reporter learned about me? Who had given him my picture? Surely, they must know or else could point me in the right direction.

Those were questions I desperately wanted answered.

"Good afternoon," a chipper woman in her thirties told me from behind the front desk. "How can I help you today?"

"I'm looking for Mr. Taylor Rossen. Is he available?"

"Mr. Taylor Rossen?" the receptionist repeated, confused. "Do you mean Ms. Taylor Rossen, the beat reporter?"

He was a she. The paper had failed to put a "Ms." or "Mr." in front of their name.

"That's right. Is she in? I'd like to have a word with her."

The receptionist typed a few commands into her computer.

"I can see if she's at her desk today. Just a moment."

A few buttons were pressed on the phone as the woman's headset was adjusted.

"Ms. Rossen? There's someone here to... I'm sorry? Oh, Mrs. Jennings. I didn't realize you had answered her phone. Yes. Yes, there's a gentleman here to see Ms. Rossen. When is she due back? I see. I will let him know. Thank you."

The receptionist touched the side of her headset and then looked up at me.

"Ms. Rossen is covering an event over at Cookbook Nook. Ms. Cooper is holding a meet-and-greet for a well-known cookbook author right now. Taylor is there covering the event with a photographer."

"Cookbook Nook, huh? Can you tell me where that is?"

"It's on the corner of 3rd and Main. The building is big and purple. You can't miss it."

I thanked the woman and headed back to my Jeep. Sherlock greeted me with a lick on my hand.

"We're off to Cookbook Nook," I told the inquisitive corgi. "Apparently this town doesn't have any cable, but they have a whole store dedicated to cookbooks. Let's go check it out, okay?"

The receptionist was right. It was big, purple, and very hard to miss. I didn't know who this author was who was holding this book signing, but clearly, they were well known. There wasn't a parking space to be had anywhere within a half mile of the place. I looked down at Sherlock as I parked the Jeep. I really didn't want to leave him unattended for that long. Was the store pet friendly? A quick search on Google located the store's Facebook page. Turns out the answer was yes and no. Yes, the store was pet friendly, but animals were not allowed to go upstairs where the store's little café was.

That'd work for me. Sherlock and I headed out.

The door chimed loudly as we entered the specialty book store. Right away I noticed the store was bright, cheerful, and very clean. As my eyes skimmed over the many cases of books, I could see that they had been neatly separated into the following categories: Basics, General, Holiday, Desserts, Slow Cooker, BBQ & Grilling, Ethnic, and Entertaining. Clearly someone had given this some thought.

There was also, I was surprised to see, a large portion of the store dedicated to selling kitchen accessories. Kitchen gadgets, cooking and bakeware, cake decorating supplies, and so on, were spread out across a number of racks and end caps. On the immediate right of the main doors was a set of stairs leading up to the café on the second floor. I didn't know what they were cooking up there, but it certainly smelled good. Even Sherlock's nose lifted as he detected the wonderful scents filtering down from above.

Several folding tables had been set out in the center of the store. A crowd of people was standing around the tables as someone, make that several someones, moved from table to table. The crowds parted long enough for me to see what was going on.

It was a cooking demonstration. Apparently, the cookbook author was demonstrating how easy it was to prepare some of the dishes in his book. A second person, a pretty woman in her thirties with shoulder length auburn hair, was standing next to the author and asking questions about the dishes. Every so often the crowd would break into laughter and then applause would follow shortly thereafter.

I saw a man standing off to the side with a professional-looking camera with a huge telephoto lens. That had to be the newspaper photographer. So where was Ms. Rossen? Could she be the one behind the tables?

Sherlock and I stayed well back from the crowds. The last thing I wanted was for someone to trip over Sherlock because they weren't watching where they were going. Corgis were known as the low riders of the dog world. I know. I Googled the breed when I had been waiting to talk to the locksmith earlier today. People have a tendency to trip over dogs that low to the ground. The point is, I didn't want to get sued.

The woman behind the table caught my eye. I don't know why I looked up at that point, but when I did, I could see that she had been looking directly at me. As soon as our eyes met, she looked away. A few seconds later I saw her glance my way again, smile, and then return her attention back to the cooking demonstration.

Thankfully the author took a small break ten minutes later. Since I still didn't know which person was the beat reporter, I decided to approach the woman behind the table and find out.

I easily towered over her. She had seemed so much taller from a distance. She looked up at me as I approached, smiled, and held out her right hand.

"Good afternoon! I don't think we've met before. Jillian Cooper. I'm the owner here at Cookbook Nook. What might your name be?"

"Zack Anderson," I answered, curious to see what her reaction would be. Hopefully Ms. Cooper wasn't aware of what I had been accused of.

Jillian's eyes widened. I tried to hide the groan that formed.

"Mr. Anderson. It's a pleasure to meet you."

"I see that you've heard of me," I said, as I took her hand and gave it a firm shake.

"This is a small town, Mr. Anderson."

"Please," I groaned. "It's just Zack."

She suppressed a giggle, "Very well, Zack. What brings you to my establishment?"

Sherlock barked once. It was short, high-pitched, and piercing. As I've already learned, and should have remembered, Sherlock didn't like to be left out of the introductions.

"Sorry, pal. I'm not used to having to introduce a dog wherever I go. Okay, Jillian, this is my dog, Sherlock. Sherlock, this is Jillian."

Sherlock sat, looked up at Jillian, and refused to blink.

"He's waiting for me to say something, isn't he?" Jillian asked, as a smile formed on her face. She squatted down so that she could hold her hand out to the corgi's nose.

"What are you doing?" I asked. "If you're offering your hand as some form of sacrifice, don't bother. He's already had breakfast."

"This is the proper way to introduce yourself to a dog," Jillian explained. Sherlock approached, sniffed the proffered hand, and gave it a lick. "Let the dog come to you. He knows I am offering him a chance to learn my scent. Did you see him lick my hand? That was his way of telling me that he has accepted me into his pack."

"His pack? Corgis have packs?"

"All dogs do. Even though you're not a dog, Zack, Sherlock treats you as a full pack member. In fact, most dogs defer to the humans as pack leader. It's how their societies behave. It's quite fascinating, actually."

I shrugged as I looked down at Sherlock.

"You learn something new every day. Listen, could you tell me who Taylor Rossen is?"

"The reporter? Sure. She's over there, near Desserts. She's the one wearing the long-sleeved maroon blouse and black slacks."

The woman in question looked to be in her late twenties, had her black hair cropped short in a pixie cut, and looked as though she was fresh out of college.

"Perfect. Thanks."

"Is everything okay, Zack? Your face looks a little pale."

"I'm fine. It's been a stressful couple of days. No worries. I just need to ask her a few questions."

"Very well. It was nice meeting you. I do hope to see you in here again sometime soon."

Gripping Sherlock's leash tightly, I headed toward the racks of cookbooks that dealt with desserts. Ms. Rossen was chatting with an older lady while taking notes in her notebook. In short hand, I might add.

The reporter looked up and locked eyes with me. I saw a spark of recognition pass across her features. She returned her attention to the elderly woman she had been interviewing and finished asking her questions. Several minutes later she closed her notebook and walked over to me.

"I don't need to introduce myself, do I?" I asked as she approached.

"You don't," she returned. She held out a hand. "It's a pleasure to meet you in person, Mr. Anderson. I'm Taylor Rossen."

"I know who you are, too," I confessed. "I'm here to see you."

Taylor blinked with surprise, "You're here to see me? What can I do for you?"

"Sorry to track you down like this, but I have a couple of questions I was hoping you'd be able to answer for me."

Taylor nodded. "Sure. If I can."

"I was quite surprised to find myself featured on the front page of your newspaper. You wrote an article about me, about my history in Phoenix, and about the death of my wife."

Taylor nodded. "I remember."

"Where did you get your information? How did you get the picture of me that was printed in the paper?"

"I was assured everything was public domain," Taylor told me.

"Even the picture? Don't give me that public domain crap. It was a picture of me and Sam, with Sam cropped out. I never gave permission for that photo to be used for anything. So tell me, Ms. Rossen, where did you get that picture?"

I studied the reporter's face. I know you're going to think I'm evil, but I was quite pleased to see an uncertain look pass across her features.

"He told me that you're the one who contacted him about getting a story in the paper. He said you wanted everyone to know that you were taking over Lentari Cellars."

"Who is this person you're talking about?"

"He told me his name, but I didn't catch it," the reporter hesitantly admitted. "He said he was a good friend of yours."

"Was he, now? How interesting. Don't you think that's a little convenient? According to you, the person feeding you information about me introduces himself, but you can't remember who it is?"

Taylor fidgeted uneasily. I got the distinct impression

Ms. Rossen was unprepared for this particular discussion. Why wasn't I surprised? Well, I mean, I was, because I was expecting to hear that the informant was Abigail Lawson. Taylor had referenced a "he," so this threw my one and only theory out the window.

Taylor sighed loudly.

"Look, I thought we had all the necessary consent we needed in order to publish the photo and the article. I never realized it was done without your permission."

"If you can't remember his name then would you describe him for me? Surely you can remember what he looked like."

Taylor crossed her arms over her chest, sighed, and closed her eyes. "Hm. Let me think. Early to mid-thirties, short blond hair, blue eyes. He was very intense, like I don't think he has ever smiled in his life. He was shorter than you but taller than me."

"How much taller than you?" I wanted to know.

The reporter opened her eyes and held a hand up about four inches over her head. Taylor was indicating this mystery person was around five feet ten inches.

"Skinny? Chunky? What are we talking about?"

"Skinny," Taylor instantly answered. "He couldn't have been more than 150 pounds."

"Anything else you might have noticed about him?"

"Well, I…wait." Taylor snapped her fingers. "You know what? As a way of saying 'I'm sorry' for printing the article and publishing that picture without your permission, I think I can provide you with a picture of the guy who said he was your friend."

"Really? How?"

"He came to my office. That means he had to walk by the reception desk. We installed a state-of-the-art security system last year. The data is stored digitally, offsite. Hang on, let me see what I can do."

The reporter pulled her phone out of her purse and punched a number in.

"Dana? It's Taylor. Listen. Can you get me Robert's number? No, not Circulation. IT. Right. You will? Great. Thanks!" She hung up and then gave me a sheepish smile.

"What are you doing?" I asked.

"Robert has a crush on me. I literally just have to snap my fingers and he's there."

"What are you planning on having the guy do? Hopefully nothing illegal."

"Oh, no. Nothing like that. Robert has already gone home for the day. However, he's the one who knows how to access our online storage and be able to pull up a picture of the guy who was in my office. He claims he can do it from any computer with internet access."

"And that type of thing is even possible?" I skeptically asked. I couldn't even begin to fathom how this Robert person would go about doing something like that. Maybe Samantha would? She had been the electronic whiz in our household.

"For you and me? No. But for him, sure. He's tried to explain to me how it works before, but it's way over my head. Needless to say, if there's a way to get this guy's picture from the security footage, he'd be able to do it."

Taylor spotted Sherlock and bent down to give him a scratch behind his ears. Sherlock gave her a neutral stare and barely sniffed her outstretched hand.

"What an adorable dog! Is he yours?"

Was I, or was I not, holding on to his leash? I almost

said that out loud but managed to censor myself at the last moment.

"Yep. I broke him out of jail yesterday."

"Aww, that's so sweet of you." Taylor dropped to one knee and ruffled the fur on Sherlock's head. "My cousin has a corgi. She insists they are one of the smartest breeds out there."

"Are dogs as smart as they let on to be?" I asked as I watched Sherlock continue to eye the reporter as though he was tolerating her presence for my benefit only.

"Absolutely. They know when you're having a bad day, they can recognize certain words, and they certainly know when you plan on taking them to the vet."

I laughed out loud. It was true. Of the few times I've been in a vet's office, not including Harry's, the dogs that were brought in were, shall we say, less than cooperative.

Taylor's phone rang. My hopes soared. This could be the boost I needed. If I could get a picture of this mysterious informant then I could start working on identifying him. I needed to know how he obtained his info. Was he truly someone that I knew? Could he be related to that horrible Abigail Lawson? I needed that picture.

Taylor finished her call and looked up at me.

"That was Robert. I explained to him what we were looking for."

"You don't look happy. Let me guess. There's no way for him to single out an image of this mystery person?"

"Oh, no," Taylor said, shaking her head. "He assured me that was the easy part."

"Really? Then why do you look so glum?"

"I had to agree to go out on a date with him before he'd be willing to do it."

Oh, snap.

"Wow. Well, um, I'm not sure what to say to that."

Taylor fixed me with her piercing blue eyes.

"Just repeat after me. We are even."

I stifled a smile. "We are even. Thanks. I appreciate this."

"You should. The little turd is playing hardball. How dare he extort a date out of me?"

I wasn't sure if she was genuinely upset or was merely annoyed. It didn't matter. She was doing this as a favor to me so I didn't feel a need to question her motives.

Five minutes later Taylor's purse dinged. She hastily fished the phone out of her bag and checked the display. Smiling profusely, she held the phone out to me to show me the picture.

"That's him. There's your guy. Do you know him?"

I studied the pic. It was a shot of a man younger than me with light-colored hair, fair skin, and a narrow face. He was standing directly in front of the receptionist's desk, more than likely asking for directions to Taylor's office. I decided he had a European flair to him.

"I've never seen him before. Hey, is there any way you can get me a copy of this picture?"

"Sure. Is your phone set up to only share information with contacts or can anyone send you a pic?"

"Now how would I know that?" I sputtered as I stared at my phone as though I had never seen it before.

Taylor sighed and held out a hand.

"Men. Give me your phone."

I grudgingly handed it to her. She began tapping icons, sliding her finger across the screen, and punching in letters from a tiny virtual keyboard that appeared on the lower portion of the screen. I squatted down to give Sherlock a few scratches behind his ears. The little corgi was eyeing the reporter as though he was still undecided about her. I felt a tap on my shoulder and looked up. Taylor was holding my phone out to me.

"I need you to unlock your settings. Tap your code in for me."

I shrugged and tapped in the unlock code, making sure she wasn't able to see it. Taylor resumed her tapping and I resumed scratching behind Sherlock's ears. Twenty seconds later she handed me my phone back. There, on the screen, was the same pic she had been sent by her IT guy.

"How did you do that?" I demanded. "Do you have the same phone?"

"No," Taylor said, shaking her head. "However, most cell phones have the same type of settings. It was just a matter of knowing where to look. Your phone has been preset to only allow the sharing of data if you're a contact. I really didn't want to change any settings on your phone so I added myself to your address book and voila! I was able to send you the picture."

I shook my head. It was beyond me. Whatever happened to the simpler days when a cell phone's only responsibilities were to make and take phone calls?

It was time to go. I could see that another cooking demonstration was starting up. Taylor excused herself, collected her photographer, and set up for the next round of photos. Jillian, standing up at the table next to the author, caught my eye. She smiled and gave me a small wave. Before I knew what I was doing I was waving back at her. I looked down at Sherlock, who inexplicably looked up at me at the same time.

"I do believe I'm going to have to take up cooking. What do you think, pal?"

Sherlock panted happily. My nostrils flared. Mr. fancy-pants author had just burned whatever he was cooking.

I checked the time. It was nearly 3 p.m. and for the first time since I had moved to Pomme Valley, I felt great. I had caught my first real break! I had a picture of the guy who was pretty much the reason why there had been an article about me in the newspaper. I had to get a name to go with the face, but how?

"What do you say we go for a walk, pal?"

When will I learn not to say the word "walk" in front of a dog? All I can say is that it's a good thing I had the leash wrapped around my wrist or else Sherlock would have taken off like a shot. As I was physically pulled to the door, I had a mental image of a farmer plowing his field with his trusty horse. It had to feel something like that.

"Damn, Sherlock. Were you a Clydesdale in another life?"

Ten minutes later we were less than three blocks from what was starting to feel like my second home. Perhaps Vance would be able to use the picture Taylor had supplied and could get this person identified. I figured there's a better than average chance that this person, whoever it was, was the same person who had been squatting at my house, making incriminating phone calls, and so on.

Sherlock stopped pulling on his leash and turned around to look up at me. He barked once.

"What? Do you see something?"

Sherlock barked again. He ran back to me and

jumped up on my legs. It continued to amaze me just how long that dog's body was. Sherlock's head was nearly able to reach my waist. He nudged my right pocket. The same pocket that held my phone.

"That's a coincidence, right? Are you telling me you're a mind reader now? I was thinking about calling Vance, that's all."

Sherlock nosed my pocket again.

"Fine. I'll call him. Satisfied?"

Apparently, he was. He dropped back to all fours and headed off down the sidewalk.

I verified Vance was there. He said he'd be more than happy to take a look at the picture and run it through the police department databases. All I had to do was get it to him. Either I could swing by the station and have someone more adept at modern smart phones than I was retrieve the picture or else I could save myself the trouble and do it myself. He even had the gall to ask me if I knew the way there. I jokingly reminded him that I had a dedicated parking spot right out front.

For some reason he didn't see the humor in that.

I struggled with the phone for a few minutes before I finally found the "attach" option and successfully managed to send a picture to the detective. Sadly, it was the wrong one. Once attached, the picture proved to be a bear to remove from the message. On the third attempt I finally managed to attach the correct picture and send it off. Or at least I hope I did.

As I crossed 3rd Street, heading toward 2nd, I caught sight of someone tailing me. It had to be someone from the PD. The funny thing was, I was equal parts annoyed and thrilled at the same time. I was annoyed because it meant the PVPD thought I might slip up and do something stupid that would end up incriminating myself. It meant they didn't think too highly of me. I was thrilled because, well, someone was following me! I thought that only happened in the movies!

Sherlock came to a stop as we passed by a small diner. I pretended to study the menu posted on the door while I checked out the people directly behind me. There, about thirty feet back, was a guy wearing a black Metallica tee with ripped jeans. The moment I stopped to check out the menu, I noticed he had stopped to pull out his phone.

I watched him fiddle with it for a few moments before I thought of an idea. Using Sherlock as a pretext, I pulled my own phone out, tapped the camera app, and took a few pictures of the corgi. I may not know how to use ninety-five percent of my phone, but I did know how to take a picture.

I made sure my shadow was in sight and snapped a few pictures. I smiled as I saw the guy futilely duck out of the way, pretending to window shop at the closest store. I don't think he realized where he stopped. It was a women's clothing shop, specializing in "blinged out" apparel.

Dumb. Nothing suspicious there, pal.

I grabbed Sherlock's leash and continued on. Now that I knew Twinkletoes was back there, I was anxious to see if I could lose him. The movies always made it look so easy. I was a smart guy. I should be able to do this. All I had to do was create a distraction and then, when the moment was right, duck into a nearby store.

I looked down at Sherlock. Easier said than done when you're walking a dog. Let's see. I could do this. What sort of distraction could I create? It's not as though I could rely on the people walking around me. Most had their heads down and weren't paying attention. Besides, there just weren't that many people milling about. What I needed was…

A siren sounded from somewhere in the distance. Ask and ye shall receive, right? The wail of the siren grew louder as it neared. Sherlock stopped walking and looked around. I watched his ears rotate this way and that as he tried to figure out what he was hearing.

An ambulance appeared directly in front of me, siren blasting, lights flashing, and running red lights. I watched the ambulance drive by when I noticed my shadow had also turned to watch the progress of the noisy emergency vehicle.

I don't know what possessed me to do it, but I instantly grabbed Sherlock and ducked through the nearest open door.

I quickly walked over to a large display case showcasing several shelves of cast iron cookware. I looked around the store I was in. Hidden Relic Antiques. Nice. Sam and I had always enjoyed checking out antique stores.

The store was large, had display racks of various sizes scattered all about, and had quite the collection of artifacts. Old dressers, large heavy looking bookcases, and even an actual wardrobe were lined up against one wall. Another had several bookcases full of old books of various sizes and conditions.

Quickly glancing around the store confirmed there were several places I could duck out of view. Granted, if Mr. Metallica happened to walk inside here and look around then I'd be busted. However, if I were to crouch behind that rack of funky cookie jars and wait a few minutes, he might just pass me by.

Sherlock, held tightly in my arms, looked down at the floor and then twisted around to look at me. A look of sheer curiosity was written all over the corgi's features. Both ears were up, his eyes were unblinking, and to complete the picture, he cocked his head at me.

"Bear with me for a moment, pal," I whispered to him. "Let's see if we can lose him, okay?"

"I take it you know him?" a deep, gruff voice asked from behind me.

"Are you talking about the guy in the black Metallica shirt?" I asked, without standing up.

"That's the guy," the voice confirmed. "He's looking for you and isn't happy that he can't find you."

"I'm not sure why he's tailing me, but I'm trying to shake him. Do you mind if I hang out here for just a bit?"

"Suit yourself. I don't throw customers out on the street. Provided you're a customer, that is. Besides, I recognize that kid."

I finally turned so that I could place a face with the voice. Now, I hate to appear judgmental, but I had assumed that the owner of an antique store would be a quiet, neatly dressed, soft-spoken senior that could easily pass for someone's grandfather.

Well, the owner of that voice, staring down at me from above the display rack, was old enough to be a grandfather, but that's where the similarities ended. In case you missed it, let me backtrack. He was staring down at me from over the display rack!

I'm sure both Sherlock and I were doing the same thing, which was praying Mr. Goliath here wasn't going

to throw us out to the wolves. Or snap us in half, like
he would do to a couple of toothpicks. I looked back
toward the open street. I could see Mr. Metallica looking angrily about as he tried to locate the two of us.

I looked back up at the large store proprietor. I had a
decision to make. I could only hope it was the right one.

SIX

"IS HE GONE?" I quietly asked as I saw Mr. Ginormous staring intently at the quiet street outside. I was trying to remain as quiet as possible, because, after all, the front door was wide open.

The big man grunted, "Yup. He's on the other side of Main now. You ought to see him. He's frantic. He doesn't look happy that he lost you."

I slowly stood and put Sherlock on the ground. The corgi sank down on his butt and looked up at the newcomer. Much to his credit, Sherlock didn't bark once at him, not even when the big man came around the display and held out a hand to me in greeting.

Before I go any further, I should describe the guy to you. Remember, I said I was six feet tall. Let's just say I couldn't see over the racks. This guy could. He had to be at least six foot eight inches and close to 350 lbs. He also could have been a contestant on one of those Strongest Man in the World shows I enjoyed watching as a kid.

He had short white hair that was spiked straight up. He also had sideburns that practically covered his entire face. His biceps had to be bigger than my thighs and his hands... Holy crap! I've never seen hands that big. You could fit a dinner plate on those things and his fingers would still be visible.

The strangest thing about him, in my opinion, was

his attire. With a build like that, looking as intimidating as he did, I had expected him to be wearing something you'd normally find on a biker. Like I said, I didn't realize I was this judgmental, and I felt bad for it.

The store owner was wearing a dark green buttoned-down short sleeve shirt and a pair of khakis. I could see some type of tribal tattoo peeking out from beneath the sleeve of his right arm, as well as a second tattoo on his forearm. Same arm.

I extended my hand and shook his.

"Burt Johnson," the big man said, giving my hand a shake.

I tried not to shudder as I felt most of my fingers fuse together.

"Zack Anderson."

"Ah. So you're the guy."

"I'm the guy what?" I asked.

"You're the guy the cops think killed Zora's assistant."

"I didn't do it," I insisted.

"That also explains why the Wilson kid has been following you."

"The Wilson kid?" I repeated with a frown. "How do you know him?"

"He's a cop."

Well, duh. Why else would someone be following me?

"He didn't look like a cop."

Burt gave me a look that suggested he believed I wasn't the sharpest tool in the shed.

"They wouldn't be able to discreetly follow someone dressed in their street blues, would they?"

I shrugged. He had me there.

"True."

"How long was he on your tail?" Burt asked.

"I really don't know. I just noticed him about five minutes ago."

Burt finally noticed Sherlock.

"That's a good lookin' dog you got there. Hold on a sec. I think I have something for him. Or is it a her?"

"You had it right the first time. This is Sherlock and he's a he."

"Sherlock? You named your dog Sherlock?"

"I didn't name him. He was already named when I got him."

Burt shrugged. He moved back behind his counter, stooped to reach something down low where I couldn't see, and came back up holding a clear plastic baggie. I really couldn't make out what it was, but I did figure it was some type of doggie treat.

Sherlock's ears jumped straight up as he watched the big man take a couple out and hold them out in his hand. He stooped down low so that Sherlock could eat them out of his hand.

"Umm, I don't know if he'll do that," I warned.

"Do what?" Burt asked as he stretched out his hand toward Sherlock.

"He hasn't met you yet so I don't think that..."

I trailed off as Sherlock practically pounced toward Burt. Half a heartbeat later the corgi was licking his chops and crunching away on whatever it was Burt had offered him.

"They're little bits of bread," Burt explained, holding the baggie out to me. "Not only are they great to snack on, but they also make perfect treats for those customers who like to bring their dogs in here."

I studied the bag with the dried round pieces of dough in them. The label identified them as "Bagel Bits."

"Where'd you get them?"

"Farmhouse Bakery. They're right over—"

"I'll be damned," I interrupted, throwing Burt a smile. "I finally hear a name that I've heard before. I know where they're at. It's across the street from Cookbook Nook, isn't that right?"

"That's right. We always try to help out each other by cross promoting products." Burt retrieved the baggie and tossed it up on the counter. Sherlock watched him like a hawk. "It's the best bakery in town."

I snorted. "Are they the only bakery in town?"

Burt laughed, dispelling most of my uneasiness with him.

"Maybe. If you go, you should…"

I had been studying a large glass contraption, which looked like an oversized Mason jar with a strange, mechanical lid, when I noticed Burt had trailed off.

"What's wrong?"

"Grab the dog and hide. Hurry!"

I quickly pulled Sherlock to me and crouched back behind the display rack. I gave the corgi a gentle hug and held him close. Sherlock panted contentedly, unconcerned about losing contact with the ground once more.

"What is it?" I quietly asked, looking up at Burt.

"Shh. Don't say a word," Burt whispered. Then, in a louder voice, "Good afternoon. How are you today?"

"I'm fine," a new voice announced.

I held my breath. The speaker was close. Whoever it was must have just stepped foot inside the store.

"Can I help you find something?" Burt asked in a friendly tone.

"Yeah. Have you seen a guy with a dog around here?"

Burt nodded. "Several. Can you describe him?"

"He's tall and has brown hair. The dog was short, with black, orange, and white fur."

"Yeah, I have seen him. Are you a friend of his?"

"Yes," I heard the new voice huff out in exasperation. "He's late. We're supposed to grab a bite to eat, but I haven't been able to find him. Do you know where he went?"

I bit my tongue. All Burt would have to do is simply look down at me and he'd give away my presence.

Burt moved out and away from the counter, toward the front door. I heard a second set of footsteps grow fainter, as though the person was walking away. I smiled. This second person, whoever he was, must have wanted to keep his distance from Burt. I couldn't blame him. I don't think I've ever met a more intimidating person in my life.

"Sure I do. He asked me where the closest pet store was. Said something about buying a few things for his dog."

"That's right," the voice agreed. "He just adopted his dog and probably doesn't have much for him."

I almost snorted with disbelief from my position behind the rack. How did he know I had just adopted Sherlock? Who was talking, anyway? It couldn't be the Wilson kid. Burt had said that he knew him. Who, then?

"Do you know where the pet store is?" Burt was asking. "That's where he's headed. Head east, down Main, and turn right on 5th. It'll be the second store on your left."

"You're sure?" the voice asked. I could detect a trace of skepticism.

"Unless you know of any other pet stores that are closer?" Burt casually asked.

"None come to mind," the voice said. "Thanks. I'll see if I can catch up to my friend there. Thanks for your help."

"Don't mention it," Burt called out. After a few moments he reappeared in front of me and grinned. "You had a second tail. Did you know that?"

I hurried by Burt, pulling my cell out of my pocket.

"What was he wearing?" I anxiously asked. I wanted a picture of this guy.

"He's the dude wearing black. Black shirt and black pants."

I brought my phone up and readied my thumb over the button. All I had to do was get him to turn around, but how? He was already twenty feet away. Whatever I was gonna do I had to do it quickly.

"What is it?" Burt asked, coming up behind me.

"I need him to turn around, before he gets too much farther away."

"Be ready. I'll get him to turn around."

"How?" I asked.

In the blink of an eye Burt rushed straight at me, hands outstretched as though he wanted to throttle me. Sherlock, who had been sitting by my feet, sprang up and instantly started barking at Burt.

Right on cue the mystery man, who was now about thirty feet down the sidewalk, whipped his head around to look my way. I snapped the picture just as he made eye contact with me. As you have probably already surmised, it was my "friend," the one responsible for giving the newspaper all my details. His eyes widened with surprise. I smiled, waved, held up my phone, and gave him a thumbs up. He waved back, only with a different digit extended. He bolted across the street and disappeared from sight.

"A friend of yours?" Burt asked from behind me.

"He's the guy who gave the newspaper a picture of me and all the details of my inheritance after my wife died. I wanted to find him but I never imagined I'd find him that fast." I squatted down to throw a reassuring arm around Sherlock. "It's okay, pal. He wasn't going to hurt me."

Sherlock woofed a warning as Burt squatted down next to me. He held out a hand to the corgi, who cautiously sniffed it.

"I'm sorry," the big man apologized. "I wasn't gonna hurt your daddy. I had to make you bark."

Sherlock finally fell silent but continued to watch the huge storekeeper, in case he tried to rush me again. I patted my dog a few times on the head before turning to my new friend.

"How did you know he was looking for me?"

"The Wilson kid had just driven off. This new guy had an angry look on his face. I think the second guy was trailing the Wilson kid."

"He had to have been following me," I insisted. "I wouldn't think he'd have any reason to follow the cop who was following me."

Burt shrugged. "If I were to venture a guess, I'd say the second dude was following the first dude. You know, letting him do all the work."

"Ah. Got it. So, are you going to make me buy something, Burt?"

The huge shopkeeper smiled at me.

"No. I promised my parole officer I'd stop hassling

people just to make a buck. It's okay. I just hope the soup kitchen is still open by the time I get there tonight."

I had turned around to head for the door when I stopped dead in my tracks. I sighed, spun around, and pointed at the glass contraption with the mechanical lid.

"Fine. I'll take whatever that is."

Burt picked up the antique and began wrapping it up.

"A fine choice. You never know when you'll run out of butter."

"Excuse me?"

"This is an antique butter churn," Burt explained. He pointed at the paddles that were visible inside the jar. "You turn this handle up here, which turns the gears you see there, which, in turn, spins the paddle. After you fill the jar with milk, that is."

"An antique butter maker," I groaned.

"What did you think it was?" Burt asked, confused.

"Not a clue. I probably don't know what half the stuff is in here."

I paid for my purchase, thanked Burt for the use of his store, and stepped outside. Sherlock instantly looked up and down the street before turning to look up at me.

"What?" I asked. I looked around. "If you see someone following us, you be sure to let me know, okay?"

Sherlock pulled on his leash, leading me straight back to where I had parked my Jeep a block away. I had just pulled away from the curb when Vance called.

"Zack. Where are you?"

"In my Jeep, heading home. Why?"

"I need to talk to you. Oh, about the picture you sent? It made it through."

"You mean you got it? Awesome. Wasn't sure if I

did that right. I don't text many people. In fact, I think I've only sent out two pictures, tops."

If only Samantha could see me now. She had been a pro on her phone and could make it do things I don't think even a normal computer could do.

"I have some information for you. Is this a bad time?"

"My stereo has the hands-free option for my phone. I can talk and drive at the same time, in case you were wondering. What's up?"

"While we have yet to figure out his identity, I can tell you that our John Doe died two nights ago and was most assuredly placed in your winery after he died. We also know what killed him."

"You do? Wow, that was quick. What was it?"

"As you might have guessed, our M.E. doesn't have much to do around here. He's already finished the autopsy. Anyway, he found high concentrations of strychnine in his blood."

"Strychnine? What the hell is that? I'm guessing that's bad?"

"It's an odorless poison in the alkaloid family. A small amount would be lethal to just about anything that lives. It's odorless, can be absorbed by inhalation, ingestion, or injection, and has some particularly graphic symptoms."

"Ouch. Poison, huh? I wouldn't have called that one. This is good news! It's not like you can pick up a bottle of strychnine down at the local pharmacy, right?"

"It comes in powder form, not liquid. And yes, pharmacies do not carry strychnine."

"It's a powder? Did you say this stuff can be inhaled?"

"Inhaled, taken orally, or injected."

"Is there such a thing as a strychnine detector? How would you know if you were being poisoned?"

"By the symptoms. If you start exhibiting any signs then it'd be time to clear out."

I swallowed nervously.

"You can become poisoned by inhaling it? That doesn't make me feel any better. I'm halfway tempted to check us into a hotel."

"Us? Is there someone there with you?"

"Yeah. His name is Sherlock. You've met him."

"Oh, right. The dog. Listen, if you were exposed to strychnine, you'd know it. And I already told you that this guy was dumped in Lentari Cellars after he was dead, so I think you and your dog will be fine. Zack, did you catch that? Our John Doe was placed in your winery after his death, which the M.E. puts at around 11p.m. the night before last."

"Wait, are you telling me that I'm no longer a suspect?" I incredulously asked. There's no way my luck could be that good. "I'll bet Chief Nelson just loved to hear that."

"Off the record, he knows you're innocent," Vance admitted. "However, until the case is solved and the perpetrator is behind bars, he's going to keep an eye on you."

"What about Debbie Jacobs?" I asked. "Do you guys still think I had something to do with her death?"

"Same situation. I think the chief knows you didn't do it, and would very much like to find concrete proof that you didn't, but until such time you are still our number one suspect."

"What about you?" I asked. "What do you think?"

"I'll be honest. I thought you were guilty. At first."

"Understandable. And now?"

"I'm not so sure," Vance admitted.

"Hey, you know that picture of the blonde guy I sent you?"

"I've got it running through every database I can think of. There are no hits anywhere yet."

I took a deep breath and slowly let it out. "He's still in town."

Several seconds of silence passed before I heard Vance clear his throat.

"Would you care to run that by me again?"

"I caught him following me earlier. Well, Burt from the antique store noticed him first."

"When was this?"

"After I ditched the Wilson kid."

Several more seconds passed in silence.

"Zack?"

"Yeah?"

"May I make a recommendation?"

"Sure."

"Don't try to actively lose a police tail. It kinda makes you look guilty, you know?"

"Point taken," I laughed. "Burt said that the second guy was tailing the first guy."

"Are you sure Eric wasn't the one following your mystery guy?"

"Eric?"

"He's the 'Wilson kid,' as you so eloquently called him."

"Oh. Yes, I'm positive. He came into the antique store and talked to Burt."

"He did? What'd he say?"

"He wanted to know if Burt had seen a guy with a dog. Burt pointed him in the opposite direction."

"Burt Johnson was actively helping you out?" Vance asked. I got the feeling that the detective was impressed. "He's former military. A Ranger, I think. Trust doesn't come easily to him. Most people are scared of him even though he's harmless."

"I can see that. The guy is huge. Anyway, Burt told the guy that I needed something for Sherlock and pointed him toward the pet store. Blondie wanted to act like he knew where it was, but I think we could both tell that he didn't know. Burt made some offside comment about the other pet stores in town, which the guy didn't know about, and…"

"Smart move, Burt," Vance interrupted. "Smart."

"What is?"

"It was a trick question. Burt must've been suspicious of the guy and asked a question that confirmed he wasn't a local. The pet store on 5th is the only pet store in town."

"Ah. Makes sense. Hey, get this. Blondie knew I had recently adopted Sherlock."

"How did he know that?" Vance asked, confused. "You adopted your dog, what, yesterday, right?"

"Right," I confirmed. "How could he know that? Does that mean he's been watching me since yesterday?"

"It sure sounds like it. If this is the same guy in the picture you sent me then I'd say it's clear he's been in town for a little while now. He probably knows the area better than you, just not enough to know there is only one pet store in town. I'd be careful if I were you."

"I am so getting an alarm system for the house tomorrow."

"That's a good idea," Vance agreed. "I don't like knowing this guy is somewhere out there. For all we know he could be the guy that's the mastermind behind this whole *Bengál* theft. I'll put an APB out on him. If he's still in town we'll find him."

I turned right onto Reservoir Road, on my way to Forest Park Dr.

"Vance, if the guy in the picture does turn out to be the mastermind in all of this, meaning he's the one who dumped the body I found in the winery, would that imply the tiger is hidden somewhere in Lentari Cellars?"

"I doubt it. Why would he draw attention to the tiger's hiding spot by dumping a body there?"

"Good point."

I was approaching the front driveway to my new house. I pulled the Jeep over to the mailbox and checked for mail, all without getting out of the car. I tossed a few credit card offers onto my dash and drove toward the house.

"I'm guessing you finally made it back to your house?" Vance casually asked.

"Just got here," I confirmed. "Wait a minute. How'd you know that? Do you have my Jeep bugged? Wait. You know what? Don't tell me. I don't want to know if you do."

Vance laughed and hung up.

I dropped my keys and my wallet down on the kitchen counter. I pulled one of the ugly orange chairs out from the dinner table and sat down, sighing as I did. Sherlock settled to the ground and watched me. I pulled out my phone, called up the picture Taylor had saved for me, and studied it.

I was confident that prior to today I had never laid eyes on this guy in my life. I held the phone down to show Sherlock. The corgi sniffed once and then looked up at me as though it was up to me to make the next move.

"What do you think? Do you know who this is? Someone's gotta know him. Hopefully Vance will be able to…"

I trailed off as I watched Sherlock rise to his feet and trot out of the room, as though he had someplace to be. Bemused, I set out after him. I found him settling down onto the bed in the master bedroom. He wasn't acting tired, nor was he acting like he was planning on taking a doggie nap, but he was lying down. In fact, his head was resting on his two front paws as he returned my stare.

"What are we in here for, pal? Are you tired? Do you want to take a nap?"

I kicked my shoes off and moved to the dresser. I slipped my wedding band off and set it in the box Samantha had originally presented it to me in. For some reason I couldn't bring myself to not wear my ring. I had tried for a few days, but my left hand had ended up feeling bare; naked. I couldn't do it. Not only that, I had felt supremely guilty the entire time, like I had been unfaithful. I know I shouldn't be. Samantha was dead and gone. I couldn't—and shouldn't—keep dwelling on the past. Nevertheless, until I could feel comfortable taking the ring off and not breaking out in a cold sweat, the ring would stay where it belonged, which was on my finger. However, once I was home, the ring belonged in its holder on my dresser, plain and simple.

I was heading back around the bed when one of my feet collided with a corner of the heavy wood bed frame. The pain was so bad that I think I literally saw stars. I dropped to my knees and stayed there for at least five minutes, massaging my foot and cursing like a sailor. Only when I was able to see straight did I work up the nerve to look. I halfway expected to find a toe jammed all way back inside my foot, like you'd see in the cartoons. Or else sticking out at a grotesque angle.

Thankfully neither was the case. Oh, it throbbed, don't get me wrong, but at least it didn't look broken. Man alive, had that hurt. Why couldn't that have happened while I had still been wearing my shoes?

But, as I was slowly regaining my feet, I saw something that made me forget my pain. There was something hanging on the wall behind the large table lamp. It was an older picture, judging by the graininess of the image and the yellowing of the paper. And the hair.

Oh, that hair! Fluffy, feathery hairdos that must have required hours of primping and preening were found on both the men and the women. Many of the men's hair styles were just as long, if not longer, than the women's. I knew with utter certainty that the photo was from the '80s. Now, in case you do the math, yes, that was pretty much my decade. It's when I graduated high school, got my first car, my first job, and so on. And before you ask, NO, I never had my hair looking like that.

I plucked the picture from the wall and studied it. It was a group shot, with at least twenty people—including kids—crammed into the picture. There, standing just behind the woman seated on a chair in the middle, was Abigail Lawson. She may have been young, well, young-ish, but even at that age she had that same scowl plastered across her face. I focused on the seated woman. That had to be Aunt Bonnie. She was sitting, prim and proper, on her seat and had neither smile nor scowl on her face. It looked as if she just wanted to get the experience of taking the photo over with.

I started to put the picture back on the wall when one of the children sitting in front of Bonnie caught my eye. It was a boy with fair skin and blond hair. Could it be? I pulled out my cell and pulled up the picture of my elusive secret admirer.

It was him! He had the same nose, the same forehead, and the same guarded look on his face. Who was he? Could he be Bonnie's grandson? Was I being tailed by Abigail's son?

Everything started to fall into place. This guy had to be Abigail's son. He was probably reporting everything I had been doing back to his overbearing mother. My theory had been right all along. Abigail Lawson was behind the whole thing! Clearly, she wanted Lentari Cellars bad enough to kill for it.

I looked over at Sherlock and vowed again not to let the dog out of my sight. Not until this whole mess had blown over. It had surprised me to learn how much I enjoyed caring for the little corgi. It had given me something to do, someone to care for, and apparently that was something I sorely needed.

I limped back to the bed, intent on jumping up with Sherlock, when the little corgi casually rose to his feet, jumped down to the ground and trotted away. I slid the cell into my pants pocket and followed. Now what was the little booger up to? Who would have known owning a dog would be so interesting? Did all dogs behave this way?

Sherlock retraced his steps back to the utility room. He scratched at the closed door once and turned to look at me.

"If you will allow me, your majesty."

Sherlock trotted through the newly opened door and looked back to make sure I followed.

"I'm still here. What do you want to show me now?"

Sherlock sat, looked around the room, sighed, and slid into a down position.

"There's nothing here. Come on. We've got other things to do."

The corgi didn't budge. He remained on the floor, motionless, and blinked his eyes at me.

"What? What do you want now? Is there something in here you want me to see? Oh, what the hell. You've been right about everything else."

I hit the switch to the overhead light and inspected the walls, floors, and cabinets. Nothing looked out of place. Well, what about the opposite? Was there anything there that shouldn't be? Let's see. Washer, check. Dryer, check. Laundry sink, check. Cabinets? Already checked, so check.

What was left? I looked down at Sherlock to see him looking up, but not at me. He was staring at the ceiling. I craned my head to see what he was looking at. The only thing I could see was a fluorescent light fixture that looked as though it had been there since time began.

"I hate to break it to you, pal," I began as I looked down at the little corgi, "but there's nothing here. There's nothing up there, well, except for the second floor. If you want up there then you'll have to take the stairs."

Sherlock let out a snort and trotted out of the room.

Intrigued, I decided to follow. He headed straight toward the foyer. More specifically, he was heading to the staircase.

Sherlock arrived at the base of the stairs and paused. He craned his neck to look up at the imposing flight of steps and looked back at me. He shook his collar, looked up at the stairs once more, and then plopped his butt down.

"Hey, don't look at me," I told the corgi. "If you want up there, then you're going to do it yourself. I'm not carrying you up there, Princess."

I am ashamed to admit I tried to out-stubborn a dog. Five minutes passed and neither one of us budged. Sherlock stared at me the entire time. I don't think he blinked once. With a resigned sigh, I picked up His Royal Canineship and carried him to the second floor. Once I set him down, he was off again.

Sherlock headed to the largest of the three guest rooms on this floor. Coincidentally, it was the room I had chosen to be my office. My furry companion took a brief look around the room and immediately moved to the closet door. Before I knew what I was doing, I had opened the door, figuring Sherlock wanted to inspect this part of the room, too.

Sherlock trotted into the large walk-in closet, plunked his butt down once more, and stared up at the ceiling. Now what was he looking at? I stepped inside the closet with the dog and looked up. I looked down at the corgi and scratched behind his ears.

The two of us were looking at a set of fold-away stairs which allowed attic access. And, by my estimation, we were now directly above the utility room. How had Sherlock known this was in here? As far as I was aware, he hadn't been in this closet before now. Neither had I, for that matter.

Well, clearly Sherlock thought there was something in the attic. Might as well humor the dog. Let's see. All I had to do was to pull that little lever there and I should be able to lower the stairs into position. Alrighty, then. Let's see what we have.

I pulled the ladder out of the ceiling and lowered it into place. A waft of musty, stale air floated down from the dark opening. I eyed the corgi, told him to wait (as though I was afraid he'd climb up after me) and climbed up.

Thankfully the attic had light. Three bulbs, each with a dangling string to turn it on, were spaced ten feet apart along the rafters. Once the lights were on, I could see that there were stacked filing boxes everywhere. Many of them had labels. In fact, most of them had the same labels, identifying them as winery receipts from the last thirty years. Judging from the number of boxes, Lentari Cellars had sold quite a few bottles of wine. Did Sherlock think I was going to be able to find something up here? Think needle-in-a-haystack.

A large trunk caught my eye. Great. It was just the right size to conceal a body. I swallowed nervously and kicked the corner of the trunk with my foot. The uninjured one. I'd better not find Aunt Bonnie in there.

Satisfied there wasn't anything living in the trunk, I flipped open the lid and fanned the air. A cloud of dust had puffed out, as though I had dropped a bowling ball on a dusty pillow. Albums. I could see photo albums. This looked promising. Hadn't I just been wondering about that kid with the blond hair? Perhaps I could identify him by locating him in one of these albums.

I gathered an armful of them and returned to the closet. Folding the ladder back up into the ceiling, I turned to show the albums to Sherlock. The inquisitive corgi carefully sniffed the dusty books before turning to look up at me.

"I don't know how you're doing this, pal," I told him, giving Sherlock a friendly pat on his head, "but please keep it up. Clearly, you're better at finding clues than I am. Let's see if we can find out who that guy is, okay? Will you help me look?"

Sherlock barked excitedly. A split second later he bolted from the room, barking maniacally as he sprinted to the top of the stairs.

"Sherlock, what is it? Stop that barking. What's the matter with you?"

Then I heard it. Someone sneezed, which meant someone was at the door. I learned to never underestimate just how much a dog's hearing is better than our own. I hadn't even heard the doorbell.

DING-DONG!

Ah, there it was. Sherlock must have smelled the visitor's approach. Or else he heard something that I hadn't. At the sound of the doorbell, he naturally lost his mind. I scooped up the dog in my arms and hurried downstairs. Once the dog had all four paws on the ground again, he became a twenty-eight-pound blur of orange, black, and white fur. Sherlock was running laps around me as I approached the door.

"Be right there. Hang on a sec. Sherlock, relax, would you?"

It was the locksmith, still in his grease-monkey uniform. I hadn't realized it was after 5 p.m. I set him to work changing every lock that I could think of, and that included the winery. While he was busy pulling off the old deadbolts and door hardware, I busied myself with Aunt Bonnie's photo albums. Hopefully I could find something about that tousle-headed boy in the group photo.

An hour and a half later, I was presented with a new ring of keys. The main house's front door and back door now sported new locks and new deadbolts. The winery also had been secured with the strongest, hardest to pick locks that were commercially available. I also found out that there was a loading bay on the opposite side of the winery that had also had its locks replaced.

Feeling much more secure, I thanked the kid and walked him back to his van.

"Know anyone who sells and installs security systems?" I asked, figuring I was about to learn that there wasn't anyone in town who did that sort of thing.

"My buddy Ricky is an independent consultant for Hijinx Security," the kid helpfully supplied. "Their office is in Medford, but he handles all local installs. I can have him call you tomorrow, if you'd like."

I nodded enthusiastically, "Oh, yeah. I would like. Tremendously."

"Aren't you the guy that killed that lady from the art gallery?"

I sighed. "I'm high on the suspect list. However, I didn't do it, not that I'd expect you to believe me."

"Naw, it's cool. You don't strike me as having psychopathic tendencies."

I stifled a chuckle as I watched the kid pull away.

Once the door was secured, I returned to the dusty photo albums. I hadn't found anything about that kid yet.

Getting frustrated, I picked up the final album I had brought down from the attic. The pictures in this album seemed to be dedicated to the winery. There were pictures taken during the installation of the machinery. There was a young Aunt Bonnie proudly holding up a bottle of wine. Maybe the first the winery had produced?

I flipped the page and stopped. There was a folded paper tucked inside the clear film next to a picture of Bonnie and several children. Her kids? It had to be. I studied the picture up close. Yes, there was Abigail, only this was the youngest version of her I had ever seen. She might have been a teenager in the photo, but she sure didn't look any different. She bore the same scowl and the same stern body language then as she did now. In the photo she was holding a young boy on her hip. A younger sibling, perhaps? Or was it Abigail's son? I couldn't tell. The boy was facing away from the camera. I slid the picture out of the album and turned it over, hoping it'd have some type of identification on the back. It didn't. Figures.

I also retrieved the paper and unfolded it. It was a hand-written letter. Had I found a clue? I looked down at Sherlock and shook my head.

Fine.

Had Sherlock found another clue? I took the letter over to the closest armchair and sat down. Sherlock jumped up on my lap and curled up. I have to admit, I was really starting to like dogs.

September 25th, 1994
Mother,
Why will you not listen to reason? Have I not made it clear how much the Garno Corporation was offering? You would never have to work again. None of us would. Our family's financial troubles would be over.

I understand you want to keep the winery in the family. I can respect that, Mother, I really can. However, I worry about you being in that house all by yourself. You need your family to take care of you. I have already told you that I have arranged for a caregiver to see to your every need. All you have to do is sign the contracts that I have enclosed and you'll be a very rich woman.

At the very least, let me speak on your behalf. Make me a full partner in Lentari Cellars and let me take some of the burden off of you. Why you'd trust the day-to-day management of the winery to that foolish boy is beyond me. He has no business experience, Mother. I do. It is my place to run the winery, not his. I have years of management experience. Let me put my skills to work. For you. You will do that for me, won't you?

For your convenience I've also included all the necessary paperwork to make me your full partner. Please get everything signed and notarized and you'll finally be able to take that vacation that you so deserve.

Let me help you, Mother. I only care about your wellbeing.
Your daughter,
Abigail

Yep. I'm thinking the same thing you're thinking. What a conniving… No wonder Bonnie didn't want to leave the winery to her daughter. This letter confirmed my suspicions that Abigail was nothing but a money-grubbing twit who didn't care a thing about her mother. I was also hoping I would be able to shed some light on why Bonnie bequeathed everything to Samantha and me. Nothing I had found thus far, including the letter and the numerous photo albums, had indicated why Samantha and I had been given the estate. I'm honestly starting to think I'll never find out.

Back to the letter.

If I wasn't convinced Abigail Lawson was the mastermind behind the murder at the winery before, then I certainly was now. I read the letter again. Wow. Bonnie's own daughter wanted her to sell, and from the sounds of things, she wanted to put the old lady into some type of home!

I have arranged a caregiver…

Yeah, my rear. It's called a nursing home. Although, the letter did mention some company called Garno. A quick search on the internet confirmed it was one of the largest commercial wineries in the country, with locations all across the States. No wonder Bonnie didn't want to sell. I wouldn't want my life's work to be usurped by some heartless corporation, either.

The mention of the offer intrigued me. How much had Garno offered? Don't get me wrong, I'm not going to sell, but I did want to know what the winery was worth. And who was that "foolish boy" Abigail had mentioned? She had said it herself. The boy had been overseeing the day-to-day operations of Lentari Cellars. Was he still around? Could I persuade him to resume his duties?

Exhausted, I poured some kibble into Sherlock's bowl, had a few pieces of leftover pizza, and promptly crashed for the night.

The following morning I was busy searching more of the photo albums when my cell rang. Sherlock, who had been asleep on my lap, stirred once, and then rolled onto his back so that he was wedged against my right leg and the side of the recliner. I gave his belly a friendly pat as I pulled my phone from my pocket. A quick glance at the display had me sighing. It was Vance.

"Hello?"

"Zack? It's Vance. Long time no chat. Got a minute?"

"Sure. I was thinking about giving you a call."

"You were? Why? You didn't find another body, did you?"

I started to laugh but thought better of it. I seem to recall thinking the good detective lacked a proper sense of humor.

"No. I was going through some old photo albums, looking for our mystery man, when I came across an old letter."

"From who?" Vance asked.

"Abigail. That's Bonnie's daughter. She's the one who confronted me on my first day here and tried to get me to sign the winery over to her."

"Ah. I remember you telling me about her. Before we get into that letter, I wanted to share what we've found out about our John Doe. We have ID'd him."

"Fantastic. I was beginning to wonder what was taking so long. In this day and age I had assumed figuring out who a dead guy was would only take an hour or two."

"You're basing this on, what, television shows? It can take time for the computer to search through all the databases at its disposal. You know what they are, right? Nifty devices that allow you to systematically search hundreds, if not thousands, of records in an amazingly short amount of time? It's really far out, man," Vance added, adopting a surfer dude persona.

"Is everyone in Pomme Valley as sarcastic as you?"

"My sister asks me that all the time."

"So who is he?" I asked.

"His name is Gregor Stefans."

"Gregor? Sounds Russian."

"That's because he is. He's a well-known thief. Or should I say, was a well-known thief. He had a rap sheet three miles long."

"Our dead guy is the one who stole that glass tiger," I guessed.

"That's our assumption, too."

"What was someone like that doing in a town like this?" I wondered.

"Do you have any idea how much *Bengál* is worth?" Vance countered.

I shook my head, even though I knew Vance couldn't see me. It was just a glass sculpture, for crying out loud. An oversized paperweight. How much could it possibly be worth?

"No. Should I?"

"Try 2.7 million. Probably twice that on the black market."

My eyebrows shot up and I'm sure my mouth fell open.

"Zack? Still there? Did you catch that? That's 2.7

million dollars. In case you didn't notice, there are two commas in the price tag."

"Who in their right freakin' mind would pay that much for an ugly glass tiger?"

"You don't know much about art, do you?" Vance guessed.

"Wine and art. Two subjects I know go hand in hand, yet I fully admit that I know diddly squat about," I confessed.

"Art pieces can be super pricey," Vance agreed. "It gets insanely expensive if the artist is in high demand."

"Like Emelie Vång," I guessed.

"Right. Her work is incredibly popular right now. That makes that damn tiger worth its weight in gold."

"What was something that valuable doing in a dinky town like this?" I exclaimed. "And where were the armed guards, laser beams, or any other high-tech gadgets typically used to protect something that valuable?"

"Believe it or not, 4th Street Gallery has one of the most sophisticated security systems I've ever seen for a commercial location in a town this size."

"What? Really? I didn't see anything remarkable in there."

"That's the point. There were cameras hidden everywhere."

"There were? So then you should know who killed Debra Jacobs and who stole the tiger, right?"

"Zack, the security system was deactivated."

"Really? How? If this was a top-notch system then there should have been preventative measures in place to make sure that sort of thing didn't happen, right?"

I heard Vance grunt on the phone. Clearly, he had been over this particular topic before.

"The alarm had a battery backup. The backup had a backup. The cameras were all configured to dump their footage directly online to be stored offsite. The battery backups, the cameras, everything was disabled."

"Wouldn't that suggest that whoever installed the security system should be your prime suspect?"

"The system was installed nearly a year ago. If the company that installed it wanted to do anything then they would have done so by now."

"So whoever this is knows all about bypassing security systems, is that it?"

"Zack, Gregor Stefans is, or was, such a man."

"So who do we send the Christmas card to?" I asked. "If Gregor was our thief, then who took him out?"

"I would say whoever hired Gregor to steal the tiger."

"And do we have any idea who that is?" I asked, already knowing the answer.

"No," Vance admitted.

"Well… What about the painting?"

"Oh, that's right. Thanks for reminding me. We tested the blood."

"Let me guess. Debra Jacobs'?"

"No. It's definitely blood, but we don't have a match for it yet."

"It's not even Gregor's?" I asked. "If it wasn't Debra's, and it wasn't Gregor's, then whose was it?"

"We don't know," Vance admitted. "Do you know what this means?"

"That you'll be asking for a pint of my blood next?"

Vance snorted.

"Not likely. It means that there was a third person in the gallery."

"You're not thinking it was Zora, are you?"

"We've already verified it wasn't Zora's blood," Vance informed me. "We know it wasn't yours, since we took a sample when you were brought in."

"Which I gave voluntarily," I reminded him. "So whose is it?"

"Don't you get it? If it wasn't Debra's, Zora's, Gregor's, or yours, then the only person left would be the killer's!"

SEVEN

"So I HAVE a theory," Vance began, as he walked up the steps toward my open front door several hours later. "I think the person who hired Gregor to steal the tiger was waiting for him to finish the job so he could ambush him. Whoever that was obviously got the drop on Gregor, but not before Gregor managed to inflict some damage on him as well."

I nodded. It's a theory I could get behind. I held out a beer.

"Want one?"

Vance nodded. "Yeah. I'm off duty at the moment."

"So you're thinking the blood on that painting belongs to the mastermind behind all of this?" I asked. I popped the top off my own bottle and escorted Vance into the living room. The moment my butt hit the chair Sherlock jumped up onto my lap. The little corgi studied Vance for a few moments before dramatically flopping his head over onto my thigh. Then the little booger started drooling on me. "Were you able to check it against your databases to see if there are any hits?"

"Eureka!" Vance exclaimed, snapping his fingers like the smartass I knew him to be. "So that's what we forgot. If only we went to school for this type of shit, then we wouldn't have missed that."

I held up my hands in surrender.

"Okay, point taken. I didn't mean it to come out like that."

"Look, Zack, I know you're from Phoenix. I get it. Big city. This may be a small town, but we are still connected to the outside world. Yes, we've run the DNA through our system, but no, there have been no hits so far."

"Where do we go from here?"

"We know that the blood doesn't belong to anyone in the gallery, so we go with the assumption that whoever our mystery guest was, he or she has been injured. I've asked the hospital for a list of recent patients who have had any suspicious injuries. Gunshots, knife wounds, etc. If I hear anything, I'll let you know."

"What about the guy who was following me?" I asked.

"That's right. You said you had some information for me about him?"

"Right." I started patting my pockets as though I might actually have a copy of the letter I found with me when I knew full well it was sitting on my dresser back in my room. "I found something tucked away in an old photo album. If I didn't have a sack of potatoes on my lap, I'd get it for you. It was a letter from Abigail Lawson. In it she says…"

"You're back on this Abigail person, huh?" Vance interrupted. He sighed. "Look, I know you don't like her but do you have to continually point the finger back at her?"

"Back? It never left. You know what?" I gently set Sherlock on the floor and retrieved the letter. "Listen to this." I recited every word from the letter, from start to finish. Vance, in true detective form, was silent the entire time. "What do you think?"

"I can see how you'd think she's involved," Vance admitted. "Fine. I've got a buddy on the force over in Portland. I'll run her name by him and see if anything turns up. Would that make you happy?"

"It's a start. What about this 'Garno' company?"

"What about it? Everyone has heard of Garno. They're a huge commercial operation that is constantly snapping up any small wineries they view as competition."

"Oh."

Vance rose to his feet and polished off his beer.

"Zack?"

"Yes?"

"Stop calling me."

"What? Dude, you called me this time, remember?"

"If I hadn't called then you would have called me, right?"

I smiled. "Maybe. You have no proof."

"That's what I thought. Give it a rest. Leave the detective work to the professionals. Will you do that?"

"Tell that to him," I said as I pointed at Sherlock. "He's the one that keeps finding these things."

"He found the letter?"

"Well, in a manner of speaking. He wanted me to go up into the attic. That's where I found the photo albums."

"That's some dog you've got there."

I looked down at Sherlock, who had jumped back up onto my lap as soon as I had sat back down. At the moment he was presenting his furry belly to the world.

"The problem is, I think he knows it."

Not three seconds after Vance had driven away the phone began to ring. This time it was the land line and I didn't recognize the caller ID. With all the politeness I typically reserve for the most annoying telemarketer, I answered the line.

"Hello?"

I knew someone was there because I could hear breathing, and whoever it was just sucked in a lungful of air and held it.

"Zack?" a female voice cautiously asked. "Is this Zack Anderson?"

"Yeppers. Who's this?"

"It's Jillian. Jillian Cooper? We met yesterday at my store."

My cheeks flamed bright red as I remembered the pretty woman from the cookbook store who had caught my eye. I flushed guiltily as I thought of Samantha. I sighed heavily and gripped the phone tighter.

"Are you still there, Zack?" Jillian asked.

"Hi, Jillian. I'm here. Sorry. You caught me off guard. Detective Vance Samuelson from the local PD was just here. We were discussing some new evidence that had come to our attention."

"Have they caught the person responsible?" Jillian asked. I could hear the concern in her voice.

"Well, they've identified the dead guy who was found in my winery."

"Really? Was it someone from town?"

"Definitely not," I assured her. "It's no one you would know. He was a guy by the name of Gregor."

"He sounds foreign," Jillian said.

"He is. Was. The detective was saying he's the one who broke into the gallery and stole the glass tiger.

Vance is also pretty sure he's the one who killed everyone's favorite grouch, Debra Jacobs. Is that why you called? Are you looking for an update to the case?"

I heard a soft, musical laugh.

"No. Don't be silly. I called because I wanted to talk to you."

"You do?"

"Yes. I, uh…"

Jillian trailed off as my eyes widened. If I didn't know any better, I'd say she sounded nervous about something, but what? It couldn't be me. She didn't even know me. I heard her clear her throat and try again.

"Zack, what would you say about meeting for a cup of coffee?"

Holy crap on a cracker. Was she asking me out? It was my turn to sound like a sputtering school kid.

"I, er…"

"It's okay. You are probably already seeing someone. I shouldn't have asked. I'll just go find a cliff and—"

"Jillian?" I interrupted.

"Yes?"

"I was married."

"See? I knew I shouldn't have asked. I should have realized that—"

"Jillian?" I interrupted again.

"Yes?"

"I said was. My wife died about six months ago."

"Oh, I'm so sorry! Are you sure you don't want to meet for a cup of coffee? It'd be the perfect opportunity for you to slip some cyanide in my drink. I'm sorry. I'm blabbering. I tend to do that when I'm nervous."

"Jillian, it's okay. It wasn't your fault. You know what? A cup of coffee would be great." I was already imagining what flavor combination of soda I'd get this time from that fancy soda dispenser at Wired Coffee & Café. "Would you like to meet at the coffee shop?"

"If it's okay with you, I'd rather go to Gary's. I need to pick up a few things."

Gary's?

"I don't think I know where that is."

"Oh. It's the grocery store. Gary installed a cute little café in it earlier this year. His girls make the best coffee."

Ah. Gary's Grocery. At least I knew where it was.

"When would you like to meet?" I asked, surprised to discover I hadn't felt this nervous on the phone since I was back in high school working up the nerve to call a girl. Samantha, in fact.

Samantha. What would she think about this?

"Would you like to meet in, say, thirty minutes?"

I instinctively looked at my wrist. I hadn't worn a watch in years.

"Sounds like a plan. I'll be there in half an hour, Jillian."

After I hung up, I looked down at Sherlock, who was lazily stretched out on the floor looking up at me. He was laying in such a way that both of his back legs were sticking straight out behind him. It looked uncomfortable but apparently, he didn't think so. Sherlock blinked a few times before rolling to his feet and stretching his back. He trotted over to the door and waited patiently for me to clip his leash on.

"Who says you're going? She wants to see me, not you, pal."

Sherlock stared, unblinking, directly at me. He looked up at the closed front door, shook his collar, and then turned back to me. Then I heard him whine. It was a soft, piteous sound. I sighed.

"Fine. You have to stay in the car, okay? No matter how much you beg and plead I'm not allowing you in that store. Agreed?"

I managed to find the grocery store without having to pick up my phone to check the GPS. If you knew just how bad my sense of direction was, then you'd understand why I felt so thrilled. For me, it was a milestone. I've gotten lost in practically every city I've ever visited. Now, with regards to getting home, I was probably going to have to cheat.

There was a scattering of cars parked outside. I gave the parked vehicles a quick once over, curious to see if I could guess which one belonged to Jillian. I could see two SUVs, one VW van, an old station wagon that Clark Griswold could have driven—complete with faux wood paneling—and a battered Ford truck.

I glanced at the two SUVs. My money was on one of them belonging to Jillian. Or, I suppose it was possible she wasn't here yet. I looked back at Sherlock, who was already curled up in the passenger seat. I gave the friendly dog a pat on his head.

"You're a good boy, Sherlock. I won't be gone long. I'll leave a window cracked. It's sixty degrees out and I've parked under a tree, so it won't get too warm in here."

Nevertheless, I silently vowed to be gone no longer than fifteen minutes. I wasn't going to be one of those dog owners. Besides, I didn't want to live in a world where Harry Watt was more responsible than I was.

I walked back into the small grocery store and automatically moved to the left, toward the tiny café I had noticed the first time I had been in here. My hopes fell. I didn't see a soda dispenser behind the counter. Great. Just great. What was a coffee hater supposed to order at a coffee shop? Anyone else ever have that problem?

I detected movement in my peripheral vision and glanced up. I saw the store's magazine rack and a woman with her back to me. I recognized Jillian's curly brown hair almost instantly.

I noticed she was reading and became so surprised that I bumped into one of those greeting card displays, the wire circular kind that rotated in place. The collision was strong enough to knock the rack off balance, threatening to tip it over. I caught it before that could happen, but not before half the cards spilled onto the ground. It made quite a ruckus, but strangely enough, no one seemed to notice. A quick glance around the café confirmed the patrons were more interested in their own drinks and conversations.

Embarrassed, I hurriedly scraped all the cards off the floor and looked up, expecting to see Jillian staring down at me with undisguised pity. My mouth fell open. Not only was she not looking in my direction, she was still reading! I'm pretty sure she hadn't even heard the commotion, let alone looked up from her magazine.

I should clarify, in case you're wondering what had surprised me so much. It wasn't the simple fact that she was still reading, but what she was reading. Jillian had picked up the latest issue of the popular sci-fi geek magazine *Star Files* and was completely engrossed in it. I could see from the open cover that it was an issue dedicated to anything and everything *Star Wars*.

Now you can see why I was shocked. I haven't known many women who were fans of science fiction, and of those who were, not one had ever picked up a magazine dedicated to all things sci-fi. Samantha had tolerated my love of the genre, but I'm pretty sure it was only because she felt she was supposed to. Jillian, on the other hand, was not only reading about a subject I had previously thought only boys of all ages enjoyed, but she was also smiling!

I briefly thought about giving her some good-natured ribbing, but I wasn't sure how it'd be taken. After all, I really didn't know her.

"Is there anything good in there?" I good-naturedly asked as I approached.

Jillian finally looked up. I watched color slowly creep into her face. She saw me and her smile increased. She looked down at the magazine she was holding and shrugged sheepishly.

"Zack! Hello! Erm, don't mind this. It's just something that I've always enjoyed."

"Sci-fi movies? Seriously?"

Jillian laughed again. Hearing someone laugh always made me smile, regardless of the mood I happened to be in.

"Hey, don't knock them. Many of my favorite stories are science fiction. I love reading about what could be, or possibly will be. I love to sit and think about what may or may not exist out there in the universe with us."

I gazed at her with what I assumed to be a stupid expression on my face. Jillian gave me a small smile and slid the magazine back into place on the display rack and nodded.

"It's okay. Some people just aren't fans of sci-fi."

I picked up the same copy of *Star Files* she had been reading. Not only did the magazine focus on *Star Wars*, but it also had a scathing article directed at George Lucas and his inability to leave his own films alone.

"I personally think if George Lucas wants to change something in one of his films then he should be allowed to do it without worrying about what the die-hard fans are going to say. Does it really matter who shot first? Although, if asked, I do think it suits Han's character better in the original theatrical cut, where he shoots first."

"But that's not the character George Lucas wanted to portray!" Jillian insisted. "He felt it was important not to portray Han as a cold-blooded killer."

I grabbed another copy of the same magazine so there was one for each of us, paid for them both, and headed toward the coffee shop.

"He's a no-nonsense smuggler who was caught by another of Jabba's smugglers," I explained. "Any other smuggler would have done the same thing. What would you like?"

Caught off guard, Jillian turned to look at the shocked expression on the young barista's face. The girl alternated her gaze between Jillian and myself.

"I'll have a blended spiced chai frappé, with soy. Please."

The girl made some notes on a cup and looked expectantly at me. I didn't know what a spiced chai frappé was, but I didn't hear the words "coffee" or "espresso" in it so assumed it would be a safe choice for me.

"I'll have the same."

Jillian turned to me with surprise written all over her face.

"Are you lactose intolerant, too?"

Lactose what? I quickly replayed her order in my

head. I had thought "frappé" would've been safe. I... wait. Hadn't she said something about...soy. Aww, crap. Had I been paying better attention, I definitely would NOT have ordered that.

"No, not really. I, er, enjoy trying new things."

Now, I know the commercials tout soy milk, and almond milk for that matter, as a much tastier alternative to the real thing. They claim most people don't ever notice a difference. Yes, I immediately noticed the difference and didn't care for it. More to the point, I discovered I learned I didn't care for chai. At all.

I took my first sip and tried not to grimace. The only positive thing this drink had going for it was that it reminded me of Christmas time. Have you ever noticed those scented candles that kinda smell like a mix of cinnamon and nutmeg? Now imagine having that taste running rampant through your mouth. I didn't care for it. However, I plastered a smile on my face every time Jillian looked my way. What Jillian saw in this particular drink was beyond me.

"What do you think of it?" Jillian asked. I got the impression she already knew the answer to this, but was curious to see how I'd respond.

"Umm, it's not bad."

"Liar," Jillian accused with a smile.

"Nonsense. Look! I'm taking a drink of it now. Mmm." I almost choked. "That's mighty tasty, right there."

"Do you know that you're scrunching up your face every time you take a sip? Also, the tips of your ears turn bright red when you're fibbing. Don't ever play poker, Zack."

My ears were red?

"If you don't like it, I'll take it," Jillian added.

I wordlessly slid the cup over to her and smiled sheepishly.

"You did say you were alright meeting at a coffee shop, didn't you?" Jillian asked. She took a long drink from her own cup and finished it off. She handed me her empty glass and started in on the rest of mine. Oddly enough I noted that she hadn't bothered replacing my straw with hers. "If you don't like coffee, why did you agree to come here?"

"I assumed they had a soda machine."

"You're clearly not a coffee drinker. You won't find many cafés with a soda dispenser. Look. I see a display case of cold sodas next to the cashier over there. Let me buy you one. What would you like?"

"A Vanilla Coke Zero, if they have it."

Jillian headed to the display case, pulled out a bottle, paid for it, and came back to the table. It was a plain Coke Zero. It would do. Actually, it could have been prune juice and I probably would have chugged the entire bottle. I really had to get that chai taste out of my mouth. Jillian's eyes sparkled with amusement as she watched me take three or four healthy swallows of the carbonated drink.

"I bet you'll do a little research before you order your next drink at a café in the future, won't you?"

"You bet I will," I muttered as I swished the soda around the insides of my mouth. "No offense, but I don't know how you can drink that stuff. It's terrible!"

"What part don't you like? The soy or the chai?"

"It's gotta be the soy," I answered, taking another swallow of soda.

"It's the chai," Jillian decided. "It has a very strong

flavor. If you're not used to it, the flavors can be overwhelming."

"Your point is taken."

"So, how's the investigation going?" Jillian asked.

I plunked the empty soda bottle on the table and felt the belch brewing. I ordered it to stay put and smiled at my companion.

"Care to be specific? Are you referring to the theft of that tiger thing, the murder at the gallery, or the dead body that was found at my winery?"

"All of the above, I guess."

"Well, Vance thinks…that's the detective, by the way, all three are connected. He's pretty sure Gregor, the dead man from my winery, was the one who broke into the gallery and killed Debra Jacobs, but not before he made off with that tiger thingamajig."

"Then who killed that Gregor fellow?" Jillian asked.

"Vance had the blood found in the gallery analyzed. It wasn't Debra's, or Zora's, or even Gregor's. We're figuring it had to be the mastermind behind the whole thing."

"But it was found in the gallery? Where? I thought the police had already searched that place from top to bottom."

"They had, but little Sherlock pointed me toward a painting that had several smudges of blood on the frame that had been overlooked. I don't know how he knew it was there, only that he did."

"Sherlock found the blood. It's not surprising. Dogs have a highly developed sense of smell."

"Well, can they smell out the location of a letter, too?"

"What?"

"Later in the day Sherlock guided me to the attic. That was where I found a letter from Abigail Lawson. She's the daughter of the winery's former owner. There's no mistaking how angry she was with her mother because Bonnie wouldn't give the winery to her. I personally maintain Abigail wanted to sell it to someone else."

Jillian giggled.

"What's so funny?" I asked, curious.

"You keep telling me who these people are, as if I didn't know them. I've lived in this town my whole life. I know who they are."

"Sorry."

"Don't worry about it."

"So, you're telling me you know who Abigail Lawson is?" I asked.

Jillian nodded. "I've only met her a few times. The first was when she came into my store. Oh, did she make a meaningful first impression. She told me, in as many terms, that she didn't cook and didn't care for anything that had to do with cooking. Do you know what that arrogant, pea-brained nitwit called my store? Dirty! My floors are so clean you could eat off them."

My eyebrows shot up as I pictured the prissy older woman looking disdainfully down her nose at Jillian's meticulously clean shop. I did my best to keep the laughter out of my voice.

"So, uh, what did you say to her?"

"My mother raised me well."

I was disappointed. I could only hope it didn't show too much.

"You mean you didn't say anything to her? Jillian,

you're a better person than I am. I would have told her off."

"You didn't let me finish. I said that my mother had raised me well. I was going for a Griswold."

"A Griswold?" I repeated, confused.

"Yes. It's a very popular brand of cast iron cookware."

A smile appeared on my face as I pictured ol' Miss Congeniality herself sprawled out on Jillian's tile floor with a heavy cast iron frying pan lying nearby. I cleared my throat to get Jillian's attention.

"I wouldn't bother. The last thing you'd want to do is damage your merchandise."

Jillian sat back in her chair and regarded me with a serious expression.

"I was ready to do it, Zack. Pow, right there in the middle of my store. I didn't care if there were witnesses, or if I would be arrested. How dare that woman denigrate my business like that?"

"She's a snob," I decided. "I, for one, will not give that grouchy woman another thought."

I stood up, bought another bottle of soda, and rejoined Jillian at the table.

"I'll bet I can change your mind," Jillian challenged. "I've got something on her that'll most definitely make you smile."

I was in the process of taking a large swallow of soda when I paused.

"Oh, yeah? What's that?"

"She's flat broke."

"She is? And how could you possibly know that?"

"A friend of mine works at the salon just down the street. She overheard a heated argument Abigail was having with someone on her cell. Your winery's name, and a few other choice words, were mentioned a few times so I assumed she was talking about her mother."

"When was this?" I asked.

"At the beginning of the year. Bonnie's health had started to deteriorate. Abigail was putting in appearances here in PV every other week. Everyone in town knew that the only reason Abigail Lawson came to PV was to try yet again to wrestle control of the winery away from her mother. Bonnie, bless her heart, never once let herself be intimidated, especially by the likes of Abigail."

"Did you ever meet her?"

"Who, Abigail? Yes. I told you, I almost hit her with a frying pan."

"No, I mean Bonnie."

"Oh. Yes, several times. She was a very nice woman. She was intelligent, witty, and contrary to what you might have heard, did have a sense of humor."

"Contrary to what I might have heard?" I repeated, confused.

"Many people thought Bonnie was unapproachable, intimidating. Not me, though. I once hand-delivered a cookbook she had ordered and ended up getting invited inside for tea. She was a remarkably intelligent woman, probably the smartest I have ever met."

"She must have had her reasons why she didn't want to give control of the winery to her own daughter," I mused. I raised the bottle of soda to my lips.

"I should have slammed the door in Abigail's face the moment I first met her. Maybe that would've knocked some sense into her. Ugh. Greedy, crotchety witch."

I snotted my Coke Zero. Twin streams of brown carbonated liquid shot out my nose and down the front of my shirt. The burning sensation that inevitably followed had me gasping with pain. I slapped a hand over my nose, hoping to minimize the mess I knew I was making of my shirt. Jillian, on the other hand, was beside herself with the giggles. She dabbed the corners of her eyes with her napkin and pulled a few more from the dispenser to hand to me.

"You almost made it to the table," Jillian observed, between giggles. "That's an impressive shot."

I glanced at my shirt. Naturally I had chosen one of my lighter-colored tees today. You know, the kind that show stains really well? There it was. Two rows of tiny spots all the way down to my stomach. Wow. That was an impressive shot.

"Did I make you do that?" Jillian innocently asked.

"What do you think?" I countered. I wiped my face and then my hand.

"What's the matter? Didn't think someone like me could talk like that?"

I tried soaking up the excess soda from my shirt with a few fresh napkins. All I ended up doing was smearing the soda into my shirt, making the stain more noticeable.

"Not really. Sorry you had to see that."

"Zack, I grew up with an older brother. There's nothing that you, or anyone else for that matter, could say that I haven't heard before. You should've heard my brother whenever he hit his thumb with a hammer."

A grin split my face. I had smashed my thumb a few times when I had thought, erroneously, that anyone could be a carpenter. Thankfully Samantha hadn't been around to hear the tirade of profanity that had ensued, thus ending that short-lived profession.

"Samantha would have liked you," I said, looking across at Jillian.

Jillian's expression softened. "Tell me about her. How long ago did you say that she died?"

"Almost six months," I answered.

"You think about her all the time, don't you? That's not healthy, you know."

"I know," I sighed. "Does it show?"

"It's not that hard to figure out," Jillian told me. "And it's easy to see why. You miss her."

I shrugged. "Of course I do. It's not like I have one of those flashy things from *Men in Black* that can make me forget her."

"Flashy things, huh? You really like movies, don't you?"

"Always have, always will. Samantha called it a sickness."

Jillian smiled, sipped her drink, and held my eyes with hers.

"What was she like?"

"Kind," I instantly replied. "Intelligent. Wickedly awesome at Tetris. I thought I was good but she was better. Way better."

Jillian let out a laugh. A small part of me had found it charming and I instantly compared the laugh to Samantha's. Almost immediately a wave of guilt threatened to wash over me. My skin paled and I had to take a couple of gulps of air.

"Are you okay?" Jillian asked me, concern evident in her voice.

"Yeah, sorry. I really need to stop doing that."

"Let me guess. You compared me to her, didn't you?"

"Yes," I admitted. "I'm sorry. Believe it or not, I'm getting better."

"How long were the two of you together?"

"Since high school. Much to the chagrin of both our families, we married right out of school. I swear that if you were to look up the definition of the word 'soulmates' you'd see a picture of Sam and me."

"If you don't mind me asking, what happened to her? How did she die? Was it cancer?"

I shook my head. "Car accident. To this day no one knows what happened. They say her car swerved into oncoming traffic and she collided head-on with a semi."

"I'm sorry, Zack."

I sighed and sat back in my chair, "Yeah, me, too. However, that's in the past. I'm doing my damnedest not to dwell on it. What about you? Are you married?"

I watched Jillian's eyes fall down to her hands. She took a deep breath and I instantly knew we had more in common than either of us had originally realized. I grunted, drawing Jillian's eyes to my own.

"What?" she asked.

"That must be what I look like when someone asks me about Sam," I told Jillian in the gentlest tone that I could muster. "How long ago did he pass away?"

"Two years. It's been two years since I lost Michael."

I saw that Jillian's eyes had filled.

"It's been two years," I said. "Is the pain ever going to go away?"

Jillian shook her head. "No. It won't."

"What did he die of? Can you tell me?"

Jillian nodded. "Sure. I can talk about him. It still

hurts, but I've learned to live with it. He had lung cancer."

"I'm sorry. That's rough. Was he a smoker?"

"No," she said, shaking her head. "He never touched a cigarette in all his life."

"Then what—?"

"Second-hand smoke," Jillian answered, seeing my look of confusion. "Here was a man who took care of himself, didn't drink, never smoked, yet contracted lung cancer because the people at his work smoked. Life isn't fair, Zack. He didn't deserve to go through that."

"You've been dealing with the pain far longer than I have," I observed. "How do you cope with it?"

Jillian leaned forward and placed a hand over one of mine.

"What you need to learn, Zack, is that even though your wife is gone, your memory of her never will be. It's something that you have to live with. You said her name was Sam?"

"Yes, short for Samantha."

"Do you think Samantha would have wanted you to dwell on her for the rest of your life?"

I automatically shook my head no.

"Nor would Mike have wanted that for me. So, I am honoring his memory by continuing to live my life to the fullest."

I looked at her questioningly.

"I've been to therapy," Jillian supplied. "It really has helped. There's even a support group in Medford for people who have been widowed. Whenever I'm feeling down, I'll attend a meeting. Trust me, nothing will help you feel better than being in a room full of people going through the same thing you are. You should come with me the next time I go. It'll be uplifting, I promise you."

I leaned back in my chair and polished off my soda.

"I'm not sure how we worked around to this particular subject," I told her, "but I will say that I'm not sorry that we did. You're right. It helps to talk about it."

"I didn't mean to distract you," Jillian apologized. "What were we talking about before we each veered off subject?"

"Abigail," I recalled.

"That's right. I was starting to tell you Abigail is suffering through a major financial crisis."

"So, she's broke," I said, as I crossed my arms over my chest. I felt moisture and looked down. The twin trails of soda were still there. The stain may be beginning to dry but, sadly, it was blatantly obvious that I had made a mess of my shirt. Oh, well. Win some, lose some. "It couldn't happen to a nicer person. So that's gotta be why she wants the winery so much. Judging by the number of receipt boxes I saw up in my attic, Lentari Cellars must do a lot of business."

Jillian nodded. "They do. In its prime, your winery was a veritable cash cow and I'd say Abigail knows it. Wait. Do you think she is responsible for the murder in the winery? Is she trying to frame you to get you out of the picture?"

Giving up on my cleanup efforts, I recrossed my arms.

"In a nutshell, that's my theory. Initially I hadn't taken into consideration the financial aspect of it. I just thought she viewed me as an outsider and was outraged that someone like me had inherited the winery."

"I can guarantee you she doesn't care who you are,"

Jillian assured me. "She knows how much Lentari Cellars has made in the past and is desperate to lay claim to that money now. She just has to figure out how to get you out of the picture."

"The winery may have made money in the past," I pointed out, "but that doesn't mean it will now. If people are waiting for me to bring that winery back to life, then they are going to be disappointed. I don't know a thing about wine, let alone making it. Have you ever seen the insides of a winery? There's some complicated looking machinery in there."

"Do you know what I would do if I were you?" Jillian asked.

"Okay, I'll bite. What?"

"There's a community college in Medford. Due to this area having perfect conditions for growing grapes, they offer several courses on wine-making."

"Okaayyy," I slowly said, puzzled. "You want me to take a class about how to make wine? I suppose I could do that."

"No, silly. Where there are classes, there are teachers. If you're looking for someone that knows a thing or two about making wine, then I'd say that's the perfect place to start. You need help. That's where you'll find it."

EIGHT

THE FOLLOWING MORNING I was standing in front of the information desk at Medford's one and only college. The city may be more than twenty times the size of Pomme Valley, but it still wasn't large enough to warrant a full-scale university. However, that being said, I was glad they at least had a community college.

I still wasn't comfortable leaving Sherlock alone in the house so I stashed him—with a bowl of water—back in my Jeep. I swear he was asleep before I had even locked the doors. I would never have imagined dogs could be that well behaved.

A bright, perky blonde girl with her hair up in a high ponytail was manning the desk. At the moment, she was helping a nervous-looking boy. From what I could overhear, the kid had lost his parking permit and was trying to get another one without paying for it. Apparently, the fee was $235 for the semester and the kid was trying every sob story he could think of to get out of paying for another. The girl, much to her credit, wouldn't be swayed.

"As it states in your student handbook," the girl was saying, keeping her bright, cheery smile plastered on her face, "the replacement fee for a parking permit is the same price as if you were to purchase another. There are no exceptions."

The kid finally produced a credit card and sullenly

signed his name to the slip. The girl then handed over a blue sticker.

"I would affix this to your windshield as soon as you're back in your car. I wouldn't want you to have to pay for another."

The kid grumbled his thanks and wandered off. Still smiling, the girl turned to me.

"Hello! How can I help you today?"

Hmm, where to begin?

"Hi. I'm told this school offers courses on wine-making. Is that true?"

The girl beamed at me.

"Of course!" She stepped out from behind her desk and guided me to a nearby rack full of pamphlets and brochures. She selected one and turned to me. "As you can see here, we have quite a selection of courses available, ranging from our 'From Vineyard to Harvest' course to our 'From Harvest to Bottle' course. We also have courses exploring the many regions of the world which are known for producing an excellent bottle."

"You sound as though you've taken some of these classes," I observed as I skimmed through the pamphlet.

The girl nodded. "I'm currently enrolled in the 'From Harvest to Bottle' course and I love it. My parents own a small winery and are grooming me to take it over in a few years."

"Is that something you want to do?" I asked the girl.

She nodded. "Of course. I'm absolutely fascinated by the entire process. Taking a simple vine, nourishing it so that it produces optimum results, and then turning that into a fine wine. Are you thinking about enrolling?"

I shrugged.

"I'm just looking for someone that knows the ins and outs of a winery and how to make the machinery work."

"Oh, there's so much more to it than that," the girl warned. "You'll see. Anyway, if you're looking to talk to an expert then I'd look for Professor Ferris. He's the one who teaches my class. If he doesn't have the answers to your questions then no one will."

"Where can I find him?"

The girl pulled out another pamphlet from the rack. This time when I unfolded it, I saw a map of the college. She pointed out the wing that had all the faculty offices and told me which one was his.

Armed with my map, I found his office with relative ease. As luck would have it, Professor Ferris was at his desk, poring over a stack of papers. I knocked on the door and waited for the professor to look up. When he did, I saw that he was probably in his mid-sixties, had gray thinning hair, white bushy eyebrows, and small frameless glasses dangling precariously at the end of his nose. His face, when he looked up at me, was hard and stern. I wouldn't want this guy for a teacher.

"Yes?" he asked, with all the warmth of a glacier. "Is there something you want?"

"Are you Professor Ferris?"

"Yes."

I waited for a few seconds to see if he'd say anything else. When he didn't, I let out the breath I didn't realize I had been holding.

"Hi. Sorry to bother you. I, uh, inherited a winery."

"Good for you."

I had to bite my tongue. I could feel my patience-meter slowly winding down.

"I'm looking for someone that knows something

about the day-to-day operations of a small winery. There are machines in there that I have no clue how to run. I was hoping to find someone that could give me some pointers."

"Find Caden. He's the one with time on his hands."

"And Caden is…?"

"My assistant," the professor snapped. "He's in the media center making copies of tomorrow's exams. Will there be anything else?"

Pompous jerk. Even if there were, I wouldn't ask him.

"Nope. Thanks."

I consulted my map and found the media center without any problems. It was a large room filled with computers, copiers, scanners, several large televisions, and several rows of cubicle-like work stations. Thankfully there was only one person at the copiers and he looked bored. He looked to be in his late teens or early twenties, was thin as a rail, and had a mop of unkempt curly black hair. I could also see that he had some type of earbuds in his ears. I followed the white cable down to his sweatshirt pocket and saw either a portable music player or a really tiny cell phone.

"Are you Caden?" I asked as I approached.

He didn't respond. I could only assume he didn't hear me. I reached the table the copier was sitting on and knocked on its surface. The guy looked up. He pulled one of the earbuds out and waited for me to say something.

"Are you Caden?" I repeated.

"Yeah. Who are you?"

"Do you have a minute? Can I talk to you?"

Caden reached up to remove the second earbud, "Don't look now, but I kinda think you already are?"

My eyes narrowed and I'm sure I had started scowling. Was being a sarcastic smartass a pre-req to live in this state? Two can play this game.

"Thanks for reminding me, pal. I hadn't noticed."

Much to my surprise, Caden suddenly grinned, as if he had made up his mind about something. He thrust out a hand.

"Caden Burne. What can I do for you?"

"Does everyone around here go through mood swings?" I asked, shaking his hand. "I'm Zack Anderson. Tell me something, Caden. Why is everyone around here so snarky?"

"I'm sorry about that. I had to make certain Professor Ferris didn't send you to check up on me. Once I was sure you weren't, then I figured the coast was clear."

"Actually, Professor Ferris did send me," I admitted.

Caden groaned, rolled his eyes, and held up his hands in surrender.

"Fine. Great. What did I do wrong now?"

"Nothing. He said you might be able to help me."

That comment had the effect of making the skinny kid rapidly blink his eyes and cock his head. "Wait, what? You don't work for the school?"

"Nope. I'm here looking for some advice."

"Oh. You want some advice? Don't ever agree to work in a school. Especially this one. Here I am, a college graduate with a master's degree, and look what I'm doing. Making copies. Look, man, I'm sorry. I shouldn't be venting my frustration on you. What can I do for you?"

"I hear you know about wine?" I hopefully asked.

Caden nodded. "Of course. Planting, nurturing, harvesting, bottling, I've done it all. What did you need help with?"

"Well, I've got this winery with a whole bunch of complicated looking machines in it that I will admit to knowing nothing about."

Caden studied me for a few moments, intrigued.

"You don't know anything about making wine and yet you bought a winery?"

"I didn't buy the winery," I pointed out. "I inherited it. I'd like to see about reopening it but that isn't gonna happen unless I find some help."

"You inherited your own winery? Lucky dog. Next you'll tell me that you inherited the vineyards to go along with it."

"As a matter of fact, I did," I confessed.

Caden stared at me with undisguised envy.

"Man, some people get all the luck. Where is it? Here in Medford?"

"No. It's in Pomme Valley."

"There are twenty-four wineries in Pomme Valley," Caden instantly responded. "And of those, only six have their own vineyards. I know them all."

"You learn something every day," I muttered. When Caden gave me a questioning look, I explained. "I had heard there were twenty-four wineries in PV, but didn't know there were only six with actual vineyards. It sounds like you've probably heard of mine. Lentari Cellars? Ring any bells?"

"Lentari Cellars?" Caden sputtered. He stared at me with a look of astonishment on his face. "You inherited Lentari Cellars? Are you kidding me?"

"No. Why are you so surprised?"

"I used to work there."

It was my turn to be surprised.

"You worked there? I don't suppose you're the one that Bonnie trusted to handle the entire winery, are you?"

"Yeah, that's me. You heard about me?"

I nodded. "Only that Bonnie had a kid running the winery."

"A kid," Caden scoffed. "Why does everyone call me a kid? I'm thirty-two, for crying out loud."

My eyebrows shot up.

"You're in your thirties?"

Caden shrugged. "I know. I don't look like it but I am. Listen, are you really going to open the winery back up?"

"Interested in resuming your duties there?" I asked. I was trying to keep my voice as neutral as possible, but I already knew I had asked the question a little too eagerly.

Caden fixed me with a stare.

"Only if you can guarantee I won't have to deal with Bonnie's crackpot daughter."

"Abigail? You don't have to worry about her. I own the winery, not her. If you don't mind me asking, what do you have against her? Aside from the obvious, that is."

"Well, let's see." Caden held out a hand and began ticking off fingers. "She's mean, cold-hearted, rude, cruel, stuck-up..."

I burst out laughing as I watched him switch hands.

"...pompous, opinionated, stubborn, heartless, callous..."

Clearly my new friend here had encountered Abigail Lawson before. He switched hands again.

"…pitiless, insensitive, unfeeling, ruthless, bitter…"

"Okay, okay. I get it. You and she didn't get along."

"I'm an amiable guy," Caden said. "I can get along with just about everybody. But Abigail? Oh, she hated me. Trust me when I say that the feelings were mutual."

"Did you do something to piss her off?" I asked, curious.

"Yeah, I guess you could say that. I breathed."

"What did she have against you?"

"She didn't want me there," Caden explained. "In her mind's eye that was her winery and I had no business being there, even though I had been running Lentari Cellars for nearly ten years. I helped develop the recipes for all their wines."

"Recipes?" I chuckled. "That's an odd way to put it."

"That's the only way to put it," Caden clarified, dumping another stack of copy paper on a growing pile next to the large machine. "Every winery has its own secret recipe and they keep it under lock and key. I worked closely with Bonnie to develop the unique flavors Lentari Cellars were known for, knowing full well those recipes belonged to the winery. I was okay with that. She had them under lock and key somewhere and I had 'em up here." Caden tapped the side of his head.

"So, if you liked your job so much, why'd you leave?"

Caden sighed. He finished making his copies, slid the stack of papers into a briefcase, spun the combo dials to lock the case, and then verified that the case was locked. When the briefcase refused to open, Caden turned back to me.

"I couldn't stand the increasing drama between Abigail and Bonnie. As demand for our product grew, Abigail increased the pressure on her mother. Several large, commercial wineries began sniffing at our door and Abigail wanted to sell. If you ask me, Abigail only wanted the money. She didn't care about the wine."

"Was Bonnie ever tempted to sell?" I asked.

"Not once," Caden said. "Trust me, I heard about some of the offers that were coming in. Had I been the owner, I would have been sorely tempted."

We exited the media center and headed back toward the faculty offices.

"The primary reason she didn't sell," Caden continued, "were those recipes. She was proud of the work I had done. She didn't want to see any of her wine commercialized. She wanted to keep Lentari Cellars local."

I was briefly reminded about all those receipt boxes in my attic. Those date spans went back farther than ten years. Of that, I was certain.

"You said you've been with Lentari Cellars for ten years, is that right?"

"Right," Caden confirmed.

"Who was running it before you? The winery has been in operation for at least thirty years. I know. I still have the receipts up in my attic."

Caden shrugged. "I don't know who Bonnie used before me. All I know is what I've been personally told. With my help, the winery was able to sell every bottle of wine from each batch of grapes. We were even pre-selling. In the last two years we had to create waiting lists."

"The wine was that good?" I asked, mystified.

"Yes. We were winning contests and local awards left and right. Bonnie gave me full control over the winery. She trusted me with everything." Caden deepened his voice and added a Scottish lilt to it. "And that was when we awakened the Beast."

I snorted with laughter. "Let me guess. That's when Abigail came calling."

"She was already a pest, as I only saw her once a year. In the last two years, however, she started coming by every other month. Once Bonnie's health started to deteriorate, it became every other week. If only Abigail knew how much her visits stressed her mother out."

"Did you ever tell her?" I asked.

"I only tried one time to speak with Abigail about her mother. I was promptly told to butt out. I never tried again. Bonnie finally suggested that I take a leave of absence until she could smooth things over with her daughter. I told her that I would save her the trouble. I didn't need this stress in my life. Either she promised me that I'd never have to deal with Abigail again or else I'd have to seek employment elsewhere."

"Obviously she didn't go for that," I guessed.

"Actually, I never found out," Caden said. "By the time I was ready to quit, Bonnie had fallen into a coma. She never awoke. Abigail must have gotten wind of my desire to leave because all of a sudden, she informed me it was her mother's dying wish that the winery would be bequeathed to her. She told me that once her mother's will was read, and it was confirmed the winery would be given to her, she was planning on selling Lentari Cellars to the highest bidder. I just assumed my time with the winery had come to an end, so I left."

"So basically she was lying like crazy," I mused.

Caden nodded. "Right. Although, in her defense, I do believe she truly felt she would inherit that winery. Just between you and me, I'm glad you're here. Bonnie never wanted to sell Lentari Cellars. She wanted to keep the label small and local."

"No wonder Bonnie never relinquished control of the winery to her daughter," I mused. "I knew Abigail wanted to control, and probably wanted to sell, but until recently I really didn't have any idea why. Aside from her being a heartless woman, that is."

"Do you promise you won't ever sell?" Caden seriously asked, dropping his voice so it wouldn't be overheard.

"No intentions whatsoever," I confirmed. "I inherited the winery due to my late wife's connection with the family. I'm going to keep it running in her memory."

Caden extended his hand.

"Then you've got yourself a deal. Let's get Lentari Cellars back on the map. You do understand that I'll have to wait until we start turning a profit before I return to work full-time, don't you? I have to do what's best for me."

"I completely understand."

We shook on it.

"Hey, I just thought of something," Caden said. "Would you be amenable to me holding a class or two out at the winery? They're looking for someone to teach next semester's 'From Harvest to Bottle' class and I know Professor Ferris doesn't want to teach it again. However, he knows I do want to teach the class so he'd take it just to spite me."

"Can you teach it better than Mr. Grouch?" I asked, certain I already knew the answer.

"Not only could I teach that class blindfolded," Caden confirmed, "but I could also offer practical, hands-on experience at a real, working winery. Ferris could never offer that. Too many people think he's an egotistical jerk. What do you say?"

"I'd say he's an egotistical jerk, too."

"No, I mean, would you let me teach a class there?"

Grinning, I took Caden's hand and gave it another firm shake.

"I knew what you meant the first time. You've got yourself a deal, pal."

I returned to my Jeep, started it up, and gave Sherlock a friendly pat on the head. Only then did the corgi crack open an eye. He regarded me for a few seconds, opened his other eye, stretched, and rose to a sitting position. He panted contentedly as he watched the passing scenery.

The weather was absolutely gorgeous. The sun had finally broken through the thick cloud cover and the temperatures started to rise. Ten minutes later I was looking at a fairly cloudless sky. I don't mind the rain. Don't get me wrong. However, I would like to see that pretty ball of fire in the sky, known as the sun, from time to time.

As a result, I had all the windows in my Jeep rolled down. All except for Sherlock's, that is. I had his rolled about half-way down and left it there. I had to set the window locks in place because just as we were pulling back into PV, I happened to glance over at my passenger to see how he was doing and nearly had a heart attack.

The window had been rolled all the way down and the little corgi was standing up on his hind legs, resting his front paws on the door. He had stuck his head out the window and, as much of his body as he could. Apparently, he enjoyed having the wind ruffling the fur on his face.

After pulling him inside and rolling the window back up, leaving just enough for him to stick the tip of his snout through, I allowed my pulse to return to normal. We had just turned onto Main Street when I noticed the window was down again. Okay, the first time might have been me, since I had rolled all the other windows down. The second time was definitely him. Sherlock had apparently figured out if he pressed his paw down on a specific spot on the door panel then the window would magically retract into the door.

Little snot. Thanks to that unplanned heart attack your window is going to remain in the upright and locked position for the duration of the flight. I smirked at the dog as I jabbed my finger down on the window lock button.

Sure enough, I heard a few clicks as Sherlock shuffled his feet around, looking for the magical window opener. After a few moments he gave up and was content to stick his nose through the small crack I left in the window for him.

I saw the familiar purple building comprising Jillian's store and immediately took my foot off the gas, allowing the Jeep to coast into a parking space in front of Cookbook Nook. Jillian was the one who had pointed me toward the college. I figured the least I could do was inform her how well it went and let her know I had found the person responsible for running the winery in the past.

Sherlock noticed the Jeep had come to a halt and whined enthusiastically. He knew I had made an unplanned stop and was making it blatantly obvious that he fully expected to chaperone my every move. He waited patiently by the door as I walked around my Jeep to help His Royal Highness to the ground.

Together we walked into Cookbook Nook. The door chimed softly, announcing our presence. Within a few moments, Jillian appeared from behind one of her racks of books and beamed a smile at me.

"Zack! What a pleasant surprise. What can I do for you today?"

"I thought you'd like to know that, thanks to you, I now know who has been running Lentari Cellars."

Jillian shelved the book she was holding and approached.

"That's wonderful news! Who was it? Oh, I'm sorry. Hello, Sherlock. And, how are you doing today, you handsome boy?"

Sherlock had allowed himself to slide into a "down" position and was watching Jillian like a hawk. For some reason I was reminded to pick up a bag of doggie treats to keep in my Jeep. As if she was reading my mind, Jillian hurried back to the counter, fumbled around for just a bit, and returned with a familiar baggie of canine goodies. She held a rounded piece of dough out to Sherlock, who instantly snapped it up.

"So, I'm dying to know. Was it a professor at the college?"

"Assistant professor," I answered. "It was a guy by the name of Caden Burne. Apparently, the head of that department, Professor Ferris, is a major grouch. I honestly feel sorry for his students. I told him what I was hoping to do and he pointed me toward his assistant, who practically leapt at the chance of taking over responsibilities at the winery again. I'm even going to let him teach a hands-on class at the winery."

"Now that would be a class worth taking," Jillian mused. "I couldn't think of a better way to learn how to make wine than from someone who knows what they're doing inside a real, working winery."

"My sentiments exactly."

A cricket chirped loudly nearby. Puzzled, I looked over at Jillian. I found it hard to believe an insect would have found its way into an immaculate store such as this. Judging from the look on her face, she thought so, too.

"Did you hear that?" she asked.

"Yeah. Sounds like you've got a cricket hiding in here somewhere."

I checked to see if my amazing canine clue-finder had noticed anything only to be rewarded with a bored yawn.

"Might've been your cell phone," Jillian suggested. "You can set just about anything up as a ring tone or notifier these days."

"I know it's possible," I admitted, "but I couldn't even begin to tell you how to do it. I miss my old cell."

"Let me guess. Your old cell was a flip phone?"

"As a matter of fact it was," I told her, nodding. "There's something to be said about a phone that could only make and take phone calls."

The cricket chirped again. This time I felt a slight vibration coming from my pocket.

"It's definitely your phone," Jillian observed.

"It may be, but there's nothing I can do about it."

I pulled my cell out of my pocket and held it up to my ear. Naturally the blasted thing had fallen silent. Jillian held out a hand.

"Let me see your phone."

I passed my cell over. I watched her tap and slide her fingers over the screen.

"There it is. Do you see? Your default text alert is set to 'cricket'."

I stared at the phone as though it was a piece of alien technology that had been found in Roswell, New Mexico.

"I will swear to you on my grandfather's grave that I have never messed with those settings. I didn't even know those settings were there. Why in the world would my phone be preset to sound like a bug? I've never heard it do that before."

Jillian smiled. "Well, the default sound is actually a simple ding and it is right next to the 'cricket'. Since you don't like the cricket, I could change it to the bell, chime, horn, swish, swoosh…"

"Seriously?"

"Oh, I'm not done. There's also tweet, glass, fanfare, and choo choo, just to name a few. Those are the classics. Then there's…"

"Okay, okay," I interrupted. "I get it."

"Would you like me to leave it on the cricket?"

I shrugged. "Sure, I guess. Now that I know my phone is the culprit, I'll know what to do if I hear it again."

"You have a text message," Jillian said, turning my phone's display around to show me. "That's what the number means next to that little speech bubble doohickey right there."

I tapped the screen and together Jillian and I watched the message appear. It was from Vance.

Heard from buddy in Portland. No record on Abigail Lawson. Sorry.

Jillian sighed. "Well, that's disappointing."

Surprised, I turned to Jillian. "Why? You wanted Abigail Lawson to have a criminal record?"

Jillian giggled. "Wouldn't that have been great? I would have loved to have seen a couple of DUIs, or maybe a domestic violence charge, or something like that. Man, what does a girl have to do in order to catch a break around here?"

I laughed. I was really starting to like this woman. There's something to be said about someone who can make another person laugh regardless of the circumstances.

I was in the process of putting my phone away when I accidentally brushed one of the other icons on my phone's home screen. A picture immediately appeared and expanded to fit the screen.

"Whoops, sorry. I must've touched the picture program. Hold on a sec. I'll just clear that off of there."

Jillian was gazing at the screen. It was the picture from the security footage of my mystery guest taken at the newspaper office.

"There's someone I haven't seen in a while."

I had just cleared the picture from my phone when I froze.

"Wait. You've seen that guy before? Where? When? Who was he?"

"I've lived in this town my entire life," Jillian reminded me. She gestured at my phone. "I will admit I haven't seen him in a while, but I do remember him."

I opened the picture back up and stared at the pale guy with the blonde hair.

"This guy? You're sure?"

Jillian nodded. "It's been a few years but yes, I'm sure."

"Who is it?"

"That's Gerald Lumen if I'm not mistaken."

"Lumen? Wait. Isn't that Zora's last name?"

"Yes. They're related. She's his cousin, a few times removed. Don't quote me on that. I could be wrong."

"Damn," I swore. Sherlock looked up at me and growled softly.

"What's the matter?" Jillian asked, concerned.

"Once more my theory has been thrown out the window. I thought for certain this guy, Gerald, was Abigail's son."

Jillian nodded again.

"Well, then you'd be right. Gerald is Abigail's son."

"He is? But you just said…that would make…do you mean Zora and Abigail are—"

"Related?" Jillian asked, finishing my sentence for me. "Yes. Didn't you know? They're family."

NINE

FIFTEEN MINUTES LATER Sherlock and I were at the counter watching Jillian sketch out a diagram on a blank sheet of paper. She added a few more boxes, gave them labels, drew some lines connecting them to other boxes, and then slid the paper over to me.

"As far as I can tell, this should cover it." Jillian tapped the box at the top of the page. There was a tiny "Bonnie" written inside. "Here's Bonnie. Right next to her is her brother. I forget what his name was. Frederick? I think that's it. Anyway, I know Frederick had several children. The only one I personally know is Zora."

"Bonnie and Zora are related," I mumbled. "Who would've known? So that makes Abigail and Zora cousins."

"If you ever want to get on Abigail's nerves," Jillian said, "just remind her of that little fact."

"I take it she and Zora don't get along?"

Jillian let out a laugh. "Oh, heavens no. Even though Zora is somewhat quirky, she does own and operate her own art gallery. It might not look like it, but she does amazingly well. She easily pulls in seven figures every year."

My mouth dropped open with surprise.

"Morticia does that well? I never knew."

"Morticia?"

I gave Jillian a sheepish grin. "Sorry. That was rude.

I thought of Morticia Addams the first time I laid eyes on Zora."

"You shouldn't judge her," Jillian scolded. "Everyone thinks she's eccentric. No one can explain why 4th Street Gallery does so well, but year after year people flock to her store."

"She got me to buy a painting," I admitted.

"You bought a painting from Zora?" Jillian asked, curious. "Which one? You don't strike me as an art lover."

"I'm not, but Zora wouldn't take no for an answer. To tell you the truth she was creeping me out and I just wanted to get out of there."

"So what painting did you buy?" Jillian wanted to know.

"I don't know. Some ugly thing that looks as though it belongs in my grandmother's house. Oh, you should also know that it's now down at the police department. That's the painting Sherlock picked out."

Jillian looked down at Sherlock, who chose that moment to look up at her.

"Why? Was that the painting they found blood on?"

I pointed down at the corgi.

"That's the painting that he found the blood on," I corrected. "I didn't see it until Zora had taken it down from the wall and was about ready to wrap it up, or whatever else happens to a painting once it has been sold."

Jillian squatted next to Sherlock and scratched behind his ears.

"Aren't you the cutest, smartest doggie in the whole world?"

Sherlock rose to his feet, his stump wagging happily

away. I looked back at the genealogy sheet Jillian had drawn up and tapped a row of boxes near Zora's name.

"Who is this? You have 'sister' here and 'daughter' there. Then this box over here just has an 'E' in it. No lines. Who's that?"

Jillian smiled and shrugged. "That's my own personal theory and I'm ninety-nine percent certain I'm right."

"About what?" I wanted to know.

"About a question that's been bothering me for quite some time now. You see this 'E'? It stands for Emily."

"Okay. So, what's the problem?"

"Oh, you probably know her by her married name. Emelie Vång."

My eyebrows shot up. I looked down at the boxes surrounding the lone, unattached box and frowned.

"So what's the connection? I will admit that I had my suspicions why a world famous glass artist would have ties to a small town like this. Do you know how she fits in to all of this?"

"It's a theory that happens to fit the facts," Jillian admitted. "However, I believe if you look at all the facts, then you'll see that I'm right."

"Have you met her before?" I asked. "You say you've lived in this town all your life. Couldn't you just ask her?"

"I have met her a few times," Jillian confirmed, "and have seen her around town over the years. I don't personally know her, I'm afraid. I do know that she doesn't live in PV."

"I need to study that picture again," I quietly mused.

"What picture?" Jillian asked.

"What? Oh, sorry. I was just mumbling to myself.

Sherlock found an old family picture of Bonnie and her kids. Gerald was in it, which is why I think Scooby-Doo here wanted me to see it."

Sherlock's head lifted and he regarded me with a neutral look.

"Sorry," I immediately apologized. "Corgis are much better than Great Danes. What was I thinking?"

Sherlock let out a snort and lowered his head back down to rest on his front paws.

"You're really enjoying being a dog owner, aren't you?" Jillian observed. "I can tell. You two obviously get along great together."

"I wouldn't have thought it possible," I admitted, "but I am enjoying having him around. That little dog is turning me into a dog lover."

"So, with regard to this picture, are you thinking Sherlock guided you because he wanted you to see that Gerald was in it?"

I nodded. "I do. That's the only logical assumption I can make. Bonnie was there, as was Abigail, and a whole bunch of other people that I have never seen before. I brought down some photo albums from the attic in the hopes that I could identify some of them, but I haven't had the chance to do that."

"Oh? Why not?"

"Oh, I don't know. Been trying to solve a mystery before I take the rap for someone else's crimes. Nothing major, I will admit."

Jillian giggled, then turned pensive.

"Would you like me to look at that picture? If you need some help identifying anyone, I'm the one to ask."

I briefly thought of the condition I had left the house in. Was it clean? It couldn't be that bad. I hadn't owned the house that long. Wait. Sherlock had played tug-of-war with an old magazine and had left bits and pieces everywhere. That, in itself, wasn't too bad.

"I would appreciate the help," I said. "If you could..." Now I remembered. The laundry. Sherlock had dragged several pieces of dirty clothes across the house and I had yet to pick them up. I could have just gathered everything back together and dumped them in the laundry room, only I was in a rush to get out to Medford and the college. Plus there were dishes in the sink, the bathroom had yet to be cleaned, and—

"It's okay," Jillian hastily said, interrupting my thoughts and mistaking my hesitation for reluctance. "Perhaps you could bring the picture here?"

"Sorry. I have no objections about you coming over," I clarified, "other than the house not being tidy. I haven't had a chance to properly clean it."

Smiling again, Jillian waved off my concerns.

"Don't worry about your house, Zack. I just want to help. I like you. I think what they're doing to you is wrong. Pomme Valley hasn't been very welcoming to you since you moved here and I'd like to help make things right."

I smiled at Jillian, surprised to feel a flush of warmth spread across my face. I mentally groaned and ordered myself not to roll my eyes. There definitely was an attraction here, no doubt about it. I just wasn't ready to start a relationship. Any relationship. Every time I thought about being with someone besides Sam, an overwhelming sense of guilt would inevitably wash over me, resulting in my becoming somewhat nauseated. I could only hope those feelings would pass with time or else I was literally going to have to seek professional help.

I wasn't going to let that happen. Samantha wouldn't want that for me. I was determined to live my life. I would...

"You have a lot going on in there," Jillian observed, snapping me out of my reverie. "Would you care to share?"

I shook my head. "Would you like me to give you a ride or would you like to follow me out to my place?"

Thirty minutes later I parked in front of my garage. Jillian pulled her maroon SUV up next to my Jeep and parked. She exited her car, took off her sunglasses, and tossed them back inside before locking the door. She turned around and took a deep breath, letting the air slowly escape from her lungs.

"Oh, I love that smell."

I gave a cautious sniff.

"What smell?"

"Fresh earth, growing plants, and mulch."

I sniffed again. It smelled like the general outdoors to me. My face must have conveyed that.

"I've always enjoyed gardening," Jillian explained, as she followed me up the porch steps. Sherlock was already waiting for us. "I guess I get it from my mother. She's always loved gardening, as did her mother. My grandmother was known for her flowers. She won awards, she... I'm so sorry. I'm babbling again, aren't I?"

"There's no reason for you to be nervous," I assured her. "You're just here to identify some stodgy grumps in a picture."

"I hate to be the one to point this out, but wasn't there a dead body found in your winery?" Jillian asked.

I shrugged as I set my keys on the coffee table in the living room.

"You have me there. Although I'll have you know that he wasn't killed here."

"But the body was dumped here," Jillian reminded me.

"True. Wait right here. The picture is in the master bedroom."

"What's the matter?" Jillian teased. "You don't want me to see the disheveled mess your room is in?"

Sherlock followed me across the room but stopped in the doorway. From that vantage point he could still watch me but also be able to keep an eye on Jillian, too. I shook my head. Unbelievable.

All these years I had seriously underestimated how intelligent dogs could be. The little corgi had situated himself in the one place in the house where he could still watch the two of us, even though we were in different rooms. I eyed my unmade bed and piles of dirty clothes scattered across the room. For the next ten seconds I became the world's best soccer player and kicked everything under the bed. Sherlock darted inside the room, wiggled under the bed, and began to pull things back out. After a quick tug-of-war with a pair of dirty socks I decided the room was a lost cause.

"You know what? There's nothing really worth looking at in here, so you ought to stay right there. I mean it. Don't move." I heard Jillian giggle.

I hurried over to the lamp and snatched the photograph from the wall, rejoining Jillian in the living room moments later. She had seated herself on the couch and was thumbing through a National Geographic photography book that was on the coffee table.

"Here it is. So, tell me. What do you think? Do any of them look familiar to you?"

Jillian nodded as she studied the picture. She tapped Bonnie's face.

"There's Bonnie, as you have already figured out. And here's everyone's favorite daughter, Abigail."

I tapped on the picture of the boy I wanted her to identify for me.

"That's Gerald, right?"

"Yes. He hasn't changed much at all, has he?"

"Who are those people in the back?"

"Well, let's see. Do you see this woman here? On Abigail's right?"

"Yes."

"You've met her. That's Zora."

I snatched the picture out of Jillian's hands and studied the woman in question. That was Zora? Her hair was pulled back in a ponytail, her eyes were much softer, her face was much fuller, and her mouth was in the process of curving upwards in a smile. There was someone who hadn't aged well.

"Wow. Doesn't even look like the same person, does it?"

"No," Jillian said, taking back the picture. "She's had a rough life, Zack. Go easy on her."

"Sure. Sorry. Who's the guy standing between Zora and Abigail?"

"That'd be James, Zora's brother."

"He looks pleasant enough," I decided.

"Back then, sure," Jillian said.

"And now?" I prompted.

"Used car salesman in Medford."

"Ah."

"I don't know who these two women are, on Zora's right," Jillian continued, tapping each of the tiny figures, "but I do know that the woman on the end is Dianne. That's Zora's sister."

"Okay. You're doing great."

"Moving on. The guy standing just behind Bonnie on her left is Greg. That's Abigail's brother."

"What? Abigail has a brother? I didn't know that. Where is he now? Why isn't he in PV demanding his fair share?"

"Because he died during the Gulf War," Jillian said in a low voice. "He was in the military. A Marine, I think."

"Oh. I had no idea."

"No one does. Abigail doesn't talk about it. Ever."

"How did you find out about it?" I asked.

"I'll come back to that. Moving on. The older gentleman on Greg's right is Bud. Everyone called him Uncle Bud. You couldn't find anyone in PV that'd have a harsh word about him. Everyone loved him. He was one of the nicest guys I have ever met. I just never knew how he fit in to the family, only that he was always hanging around the house."

"What happened to him?" I asked.

"Bud passed away ten years ago. Cancer. Now this?" Jillian tapped on a young woman on Bud's left. "This is Jennifer. James' daughter. Standing next to her is Nancy. I knew she was Zora's niece, but I never figured out which sibling she belonged to. I think I heard somewhere that Zora had another sister but have never been able to confirm it."

"What about the two guys on the end?" I asked, pointing to the two young boys who had to be in their early teens.

"I don't know," Jillian admitted. "I haven't seen them before."

Pleased that I had so many new names to start working on, I turned to head back to my bedroom to return the picture to the wall. Sherlock jumped to his feet and woofed out a warning.

"What is it?" I asked and immediately winced.

I had asked those three words to Sherlock on several occasions since adopting him. Each time solicited the same response: frenzied barking. This time was no different. Sherlock surged forward, placing himself directly in my path, and began barking at me as though I was the devil incarnate.

"What's wrong with him?" Jillian worriedly asked. "Is he okay?"

"I should have known better than to ask that question," I explained. "I don't know if he can tell what I'm saying, or if it's the tone of my voice, but that particular question usually sets him off. So let's try this again." I squatted down next to Sherlock, scratched behind his ears, which had an instant calming effect on him, and showed him the picture. "What's the matter? Is there something wrong with the pic?"

Sherlock stretched his neck out, touched the tip of his nose to the photo's glass front, and nudged it out of my hands. I barely caught it before it could hit the ground. I scowled at my furry companion.

"What'd you do that for? You almost made me drop it, pal. We don't want to break this thing, okay?"

I watched the corgi inch closer again and tightened

my grip on the picture. Sure enough, Sherlock nosed the picture a second time. Curious, I spun the picture around and looked at it.

"What's the problem? Is there something we're missing?"

Jillian took the picture from me and brought it up closer to her face. She looked down at Sherlock and gave him a friendly pat on the top of his head.

"Oh, you're so right, aren't you? You're such a smart boy."

Sherlock's stump threatened to wiggle right off his butt. I looked at Jillian with confusion written all over my face.

"What's going on? Did we miss something?"

Jillian nodded. "As a matter of fact, we did. I didn't finish identifying everyone. I'm pretty sure your dog just called me out on that, so I apologize."

A look of incredulity spread across my face as I noted the smug look on Sherlock's.

"We didn't look at the children," Jillian explained. "Let's see who else we've got here. You already noticed Gerald. The twin girls on the far right are Teri and Meri. I really don't remember much about them, so I don't know whose children they are. Now, I don't know who the boy next to Gerald is, but I can tell you the girl on Gerald's other side is Emily."

I nodded as I looked at the freckled blonde girl with pigtails. She looked to be about eight or nine. Jillian tapped me on the shoulder and pointed at Emily.

"I told you about her in my shop, remember?"

I tapped the small figure in the photo.

"This girl? You're telling me this is Emelie Vång?

I'll be a monkey's uncle. Sam was related to a famous artist. I wonder why everyone says she's from Sweden."

Jillian pulled her phone out from her purse and started tapping on the screen. I watched her fingers slide and scroll across her phone's display for a full minute before she finally looked up.

"It says here that she married a Swedish stock broker and currently lives in Malmo."

"Why did she change her name?"

"I'm told it's something most married women choose to do."

"You know what I mean," I said. "Why did she go from 'Emily' to 'Emelie'?"

Jillian shrugged. "Who can say? If I were to venture a guess then I'd say Emelie is the Swedish spelling of Emily."

I pointed at the piece of paper with the charts and boxes Jillian had drawn up and, thankfully, had brought with her.

"If your theory is true, how many people do you think would know that Emelie Vång is from PV?"

"Presumably no one but her family," Jillian guessed. "If I tell you how I think Emelie fits into PV, then you have to promise to keep it to yourself. I'm pretty sure she doesn't want her ties to PV known."

"Got it. Mum's the word."

Jillian tapped the box to the right of Zora's.

"This is Dianne, Zora's sister. See the two boxes here? This one hasn't been labeled, and as you noticed from before, this other one is off by itself. Well, one is for Stephen, Dianne's son," Jillian wrote the name in the tiny box and then drew a line from Stephen's box to the unlinked one, "and the other is for Stephen's sister…"

"Emily," I finished, turning to stare at the photo once more. "Or Emelie, I guess," throwing a fake French accent on her alternate name.

"She lives in Sweden, not France," Jillian clarified. "And that's a horrible accent."

I chuckled. "Whatever."

"So, back to the picture. That's Stephen on the right and over on the left is Emily. And this?" Jillian tapped her finger on the final unidentified child: a girl with long black pigtails. The girl wasn't smiling. In fact, her lower lip was protruding and she had a frown on her face. "This is Abigail's third child, Taylor. She still lives in town."

Rusty wheels ground into motion. The name clicked. I brought the picture up for a closer look.

"No freakin' way! Are you telling me this girl right here is Taylor Rossen? The beat reporter for the *Pomme Valley Gazette*? Abigail is her mother?"

It was finally starting to make sense.

TEN

"YES. YOU'VE TALKED to her before. As a matter of fact, you met her in my store. She didn't tell you she was a relative of your late wife's?"

"No, she sure as hell did not. Unbelievable. Wait. Look at the picture. Why isn't Taylor standing next to her brother? Why place her on the other side of the picture?"

"Taylor and Gerald never got along together," Jillian explained. "I've never seen two siblings who detested each other more than those two."

"Who was older?" I asked.

"Gerald. By a few years, I think."

"Let me guess. He was always picking on her."

"Every time I saw the two of them together it was the other way around," Jillian contradicted. "Taylor went out of her way to make her brother miserable. She was a bossy little thing. Still is, if you ask me."

"She seemed nice enough to me," I recalled. "That is, she was still pleasant even after I chewed her out for publishing my picture in the paper without my consent."

Jillian stared at me as though I had just sprouted horns.

"You think Taylor is nice? Far from it. She's the type of person that will stab you in the back, with only a second's notice, if she thinks she can benefit from it in any way, shape, or form."

I looked down at Sherlock and then at the photograph. Was that who Sherlock was trying to get me to look at in the picture? Taylor, and not her brother? Was the reporter the person who was behind all of this?

I groaned aloud. Let's face it. I sucked at being a detective.

I was reminded of my cell's unusual text alert. Phones aren't typically preset to the cricket, Jillian had explained. I know I didn't change the text alert. No one else has touched that phone besides me. Could Taylor have been the one responsible for changing the alert for an incoming text? Even if she was, what was the purpose? Now that I'm thinking about it, could she have done anything else while she had been in possession of my phone?

"If Taylor is responsible for setting all this up," I began, pulling my phone from my pocket, "could she have done anything to my phone that could come back to bite me?"

"You gave Taylor your phone?" Jillian asked, surprised. "What on earth did you do that for?"

"To get the picture of the guy who she claimed had been her informant. She gave me the picture of Gerald. But, according to you, that is her brother. Why would she do that? Wouldn't she have recognized her own family? Why pretend she didn't know him?"

"They hated each other," Jillian reminded me. "I'd say Taylor saw it as the perfect way to deflect attention from herself and throw a little heat on her brother. What better person to pin the blame on than Gerald?"

"But I caught Gerald following me!" I protested. "They've got to be working together."

Jillian was already shaking her head.

"There's no way. Now, I'm not saying they both don't want the same thing. I would assume neither one of them want to see you in town. However, with regard to them working together, you need to trust me. They aren't."

I continued to stare at my phone. I was convinced Taylor had done something to it but didn't have a clue as to what. Then again, I didn't even know what the phone was capable of doing, so how was I supposed to check to see if it had been tampered with?

"You look lost," Jillian observed. She held out a hand. "Give it. Let me take a look. All she did was send you a picture?"

"Yeah. Uh, let me think. She said she did something to my phone in order to get the picture over to me."

Jillian was silent as she considered. She turned my phone over in her hands and stared at the manufacturer's mark etched onto the back cover.

"This is one of the newer model smart phones. Its security settings are typically set high. Most of these things won't allow a picture to be transmitted from a complete stranger."

"That's right," I agreed. "I remember now. She said she had to add herself to my address book before she could send me anything. Can you tell if she did anything else to it?"

"Did you know these phones have ways to track family and friends?" Jillian asked as she tapped the surface of my phone several times. She slid a finger across the screen, waited a few moments, and then tapped it twice more. "I wouldn't put it past her to enable tracking… There it is. Wow. Do you see this?"

I came up behind Jillian and looked over her shoulder to see what she was doing. She had opened another program and it was showing a map of Pomme Valley on the screen. A blinking blue dot in the center of the screen caught my attention. Granted, the map wasn't that spectacular to look at, but there was no denying what it was showing. I could make out Main Street, and if that curve over there was 5th, then that would mean the blinking blue dot on the outskirts of town could only be...

"Is that me?" I incredulously asked.

In response, Jillian pinched her thumb and forefinger together, touched the surface of my phone, then spread her fingers apart. The map zoomed in and displayed a street level view of my house. Guess where the blue dot was?

"The 'Spot a Pal' app has been enabled," Jillian informed me. "Look what it says down there at the bottom. 'Location shared on another device.' Do you have more than one cell?"

"I've had more than one cell before," I said, shaking my head. "but not at the same time. And never one like this. I used to own a flip phone and man alive do I miss it. I got this one after the accident. Tell me, does this mean Taylor can see where I am at all times?"

"It sure looks like it," Jillian agreed. "I don't see her anywhere on the map so that must mean she has hers turned off on her end. Or disabled."

"So why can she see me but I can't see her?" I demanded. "You shouldn't be allowed to do that."

"That's why location sharing can only be enabled in person," Jillian answered. "Do you know how long she had your phone in her possession?"

"Not long," I said. "Maybe a minute."

"Were you watching her the whole time?" Jillian asked.

"No," I admitted with a sigh. "I definitely should have been paying closer attention. Why? Did you find something else?"

"Have you installed many apps?" Jillian wanted to know.

"Apps? No. Not a one. Why?"

Jillian leaned close and showed me the phone. The cell's many icons were displayed on the screen. She made a slow and deliberate motion of sliding a finger across the screen. The icons changed, as though a page had been flipped in a book. The screen was now blank. There were no icons, or apps, as Jillian kept calling them. The wallpaper was there, but nothing else.

"There's nothing on this page," Jillian remarked. She bore a puzzled look as she switched back and forth between the first page, with all the apps, and the second, which didn't have any. "A second page would only appear if there were an actual app on it. Do you see anything? I sure don't."

"Okay, what does that mean?" I asked.

"It's almost as if an app was installed on this page but was then deleted. Hmm, let me try something."

"I'm glad you know what you're doing," I mumbled, as I watched Jillian fiddle with the sophisticated electronic device. I was really going to have to buckle down and learn how those blasted things worked.

She pressed a finger down on one of the apps, the map app from what I could see, and held it there. After a few moments she dragged it to the right, causing the phone's display to switch to page two. She removed her finger and then let out an exclamation of surprise.

"What's the matter?" I asked, leaning forward to look over her shoulder again.

Jillian showed me the display. The map app was now on the second page, only it wasn't in the top left corner, but directly to the right of the "first" position. The app was in the "second" position, leaving an empty space directly to its left.

"Is that a problem?" I asked. I sensed Jillian thought this was important, but I really didn't know why. I'll be honest. I still didn't know what I was looking at, other than Jillian had done something to my phone to make all those icon thingamajigs disappear. All but one, that is.

"This app should be sitting over here," Jillian explained, tapping the empty space. She tried to slide the app over but the little map icon refused to cooperate. "It won't let me put anything in the top left corner."

"And that's significant because…?"

"The phone thinks something is there."

"Something? Like what, another app?"

Jillian nodded. "Exactly. The only problem with that logic is that I'm tapping the empty space there and nothing is happening. I was hoping that maybe the app just didn't have an icon, but still required space on the display. Wait a moment."

Jillian pressed her index finger down on the empty space and held it there. After a few moments a new screen appeared. I was looking at a simple page of options with toggle switches. My blood chilled as I saw what those options were and the fact that all the options had been enabled. I think I went from complete shock to indignant outrage in 0.3 seconds.

Geolocating… On.
Live Call… On

Call Recording... On
Ambient Listen... On
Ambient Recording... On
Rear Camera... On

"Are you kidding me?" I demanded, snatching my phone out of Jillian's hands. "How the hell did she get this on there? Look at this. Does this mean she's able to listen in on my phone calls? Ambient listening. Wouldn't that mean she could remotely activate the phone's microphone and listen to what's going on around me? How is this sort of thing even legal?"

"There's no way she could have gotten this on your phone," Jillian told me. "There are security measures in place on all these types of phones. No one besides the phone's owner can install anything. Not without knowing what your security code is."

My eyes widened. Taylor had asked me to punch my code in. Something about trying to get into my settings?

"Do you need that code in order to look at a phone's settings?" I asked, already knowing what the answer would be.

"You need a code to unlock the phone so you can use it," Jillian told me, "and you'll need that same code if you install anything on it. But you shouldn't need the code to look at the settings, unless you change a security feature. Why? Zack, tell me you didn't give her your code."

"I didn't."

"Good."

"But..."

"But what, Zack?" Jillian asked me, concerned. "What did you do?"

"She told me she needed my code in order to get my phone to allow a picture to be sent to it."

"This model phone doesn't need a code in order to do that," Jillian pointed out. "The sender needs to be one of your contacts."

"Right," I confirmed. "She told me that."

"But that wouldn't need a code. Zack, I think that's when she installed this secret app on your phone."

"Does that mean she's listening to us right now? Taylor, are you hearing this? I'm going straight to the cops with this, you crazy b—"

"Whoa!" Jillian cut in. "I don't like that word, Zack."

I swallowed my anger and nodded.

"Neither did Sam. Sorry." I handed my phone over. "Would you please do the honors and get rid of that thing?"

Jillian placed a finger over the secret app and hesitated.

"Are you sure you want me to do that? It's evidence your phone has been tampered with. You really don't want me to delete it, do you?"

"Well, I don't want her spying on me, either!" I protested. "How can I..." I trailed off and snapped my fingers. I quickly got to my feet, prompting Jillian to do the same. "Wait. I think I know what I can do. All those hours of watching TV might pay off after all."

"What are you going to do?" Jillian asked as she followed me out of the living room and into the kitchen.

I started opening cabinets and drawers.

"Look for some aluminum foil," I instructed. "I saw it on *Lore Breakers* once that a simple layer of aluminum foil will render a cell phone useless. If this thing can't get a signal, then it can't transmit data back to wherever it's sending data to, right?"

Jillian nodded. "If that's true, then that would be perfect. Since I'm pretty sure that this app, whatever it is, is illegal then I'm sure there's probably some way to remotely delete it." Jillian squatted down to open the cabinets under the kitchen sink. "Do you really need to wrap it in foil? Couldn't you just turn it off?"

I had been rifling through a drawer with all manner of kitchen utensils when I stopped, laughed like a drunken fool, and looked at my phone like the alien piece of hardware I knew it to be.

"Well fine, then. Take the easy way out."

With my phone safely off, I placed it on the coffee table as I walked by. There was an old-fashioned wall phone hanging just inside the kitchen entry. Verifying that I had a dial tone, I was about ready to punch in a number when I hesitated. I looked over at Jillian and replaced the handset in the cradle.

"If she's bugged my cell, then there's a good chance she's bugged my home line, too. She's probably the one that made those phone calls from inside the house before I arrived in town. Can I borrow your cell?"

Jillian pulled her cell from her purse and handed it to me. I'm pretty sure it was the same model as my cell, only Jillian had it in a bright purple case with sparkling rhinestones all over the back of it. Shrugging, I called Vance, who answered on the first ring. In case you're wondering, yes, by now I knew his number by heart.

"Detective Samuelson."

"Vance, it's Zack."

"Hey, Zack. What's up? What are you reporting this

time? Homicide? Breaking and entering? Someone run a traffic light?"

"Do you think I enjoy calling you all the time?"

"What do you need, Zack? I'm kinda busy here."

"What do you know about Taylor Rossen?"

"Taylor Rossen? The reporter?"

"Right."

"That's it. That's all I got. I know she's a reporter for the *Gazette*. Why are you asking me this?"

"She bugged my cell phone," I explained. "I wouldn't put it past her to screw around with my landline, either. Also, her brother is the dude in the picture I sent you."

"Aren't you a veritable fountain of information today? Be careful, Zack. Those are some serious accusations," Vance said. His voice lowered. "Are you sure about this?"

"Yes. Jillian told me."

"Jillian Cooper? Owner of Cookbook Nook?"

"The one and same. I'm on her cell 'cause I flat-out don't trust using my own."

"I like Jillian. She's friends with my wife."

"Not surprising," I chuckled. "I get the impression she's friends with everybody."

"What is it?" Jillian whispered to me. "What did he say?"

I placed a hand over the lower portion of the cell.

"That you're friends with his wife," I whispered back.

"Oh. He's right. We are."

"Of course I'm right," Vance said. "And I can hear the two of you whispering back and forth. Just tell Jillian hello for me."

"Vance says hello."

Jillian smiled and waved at the phone. "Tell him hello for me, too."

"She says…"

"I heard her. If you were trying to mute the phone then it didn't work. Cell phone mics can be anywhere. If you want to mute the phone, then just hit the mute button."

I lowered the phone and rotated it in my hands. I was looking for a physical button with either the tiny label "mute" on it or else the universal speaker symbol with the slash through it. Before you judge me, I'd like to remind you that I already told you I didn't know much about cell phones.

"These things have a mute button? Who knew? So, listen, I've got my cell here. I shut it off after Jillian found a hidden app."

"Just because you find an app on your phone that you don't remember installing is not a reason to panic. It happens to everyone as they get older."

Jillian, overhearing Vance's comment, slapped a hand over her mouth to keep from laughing.

"I'm afraid I'm gonna have to ask for that bottle of wine back, buddy," I said with mock seriousness.

Vance laughed.

"So you think your phone is spying on you? Your own phone? Have you been drinking?"

Jillian held out a hand. She wanted her phone back. I passed it over.

"Vance? It's Jillian."

"Hi, Jillian. Care to tell me what's going on?"

She went through the steps she'd taken to find the hidden app and what it contained. I got the distinct impression that Vance was suddenly paying a lot closer attention.

"How could Taylor have gotten her mitts on Zack's phone?"

"Um, he, uh, gave it to her."

"He what? He suspected her of being involved and he gives her his phone?! Put Einstein back on."

Jillian passed her phone back to me.

"He wants to talk to you again."

"Yeah, I heard him," I grumbled. "Vance? I'm here. In my defense, I gave her my cell before I had even considered her a suspect."

"When did you give her your cell? Better yet, why?"

"That's how I got that picture of Gerald, the guy who told the newspaper all about me. I gave Taylor my phone so that she could transfer the picture to me since I didn't know how to do it."

"It doesn't take long to send a picture from one cell to another. How could she have gotten some type of spying app on your phone in that short of time? How long did she have it?"

I was silent as I recalled the events of the encounter. How long had the phone been in her possession? Had it been long enough to install this secret spying app?

"Long enough," I decided. "How did she even know about that app? Wouldn't that suggest she's used it before?"

"You bring up a very good point. If what you say is true, and it turns out Ms. Rossen is responsible for tapping your phone, then that would suggest your phone has been transferring data somewhere. Probably online, to a website. Our boys in the lab should be able to tell us where. If we can get access to it, then we should be able to tell who the account belongs to and how long it has been used. Hell, we may very well learn that your phone wasn't the only one that has been compromised."

"Meaning what?" I asked.

"What you said. How would Ms. Rossen have known such an app existed? By having prior experience. This is a break that could clear you once and for all, Zack."

"That's music to my ears, pal."

"Thought you might say that. Listen, how did you know Taylor and Gerald are brother and sister?"

"Jillian told me."

"Well, if Taylor is Abigail's daughter, then it'd make perfect sense why she and Gerald are conspiring against you."

"Conspiring against me, yes," I agreed, "but they aren't working together."

"How could you possibly know that? What, did you sit them both down and have a friendly chat with them?"

"Apparently the two of them hate each other," I explained. "You couldn't possibly get them in the same room together at the same time without some type of bloodshed ensuing. If I were to venture a guess…"

"Oh, by all means," came Vance's sarcastic response. "This I gotta hear."

"Bite me, dude. As I was saying, before I was rudely interrupted, I think both Taylor and Gerald are trying to get me out of the picture so that they can see who will get on their mom's good side first. Abigail thinks the winery should be hers. She clearly wants to sell and I would imagine her kids want the money. The one thorn in everyone's side is me."

"Hmmm. If we can prove that your phone was tampered with, and if we can pin any of it to either of the

Manson family there, then that'd be the proof we would need to bring them in for questioning. Where's your phone now? Do you have it there with you?"

"I've got it here. It's presently shut off, just in case there might be a way to remotely remove that incriminating app."

"Smart thinking. Get that phone to me. I'll have the lab boys put a rush on it. In the meantime, I'll see what I can dig up on Ms. Rossen."

"You got it." I ended the call, turned to hand Jillian her phone back when Sherlock, who had been napping on the ground at my feet, suddenly sprang up and began growling.

"What's with him?" Jillian asked, looking down at the snarling corgi. "What's the matter? Do you smell something, boy?"

Sherlock barked. It wasn't the I'm-happy-to-see-you bark most dogs would typically do after seeing their owners come home from work, but more of the keep-your-%&^#$-distance-or-else-I'll-rip-out-your-throat type of bark. Little Sherlock had either smelled or heard something and was letting whoever, or whatever, it was know that they were not welcome here.

Jillian followed me as I headed toward the living room. Just then we heard something that stopped us dead in our tracks. Someone had just inserted a key into the lock on the front door. Moments later we heard the door close. My blood froze. Someone had just unlocked my own front door and come in, as though they owned the place!

We hurried back to the kitchen. I shushed Sherlock as I knelt down to open the cabinets under the stove. I may not know where everything is in the kitchen, but

I do know that's where Aunt Bonnie kept her cook-ware. I reached into the cabinet and grabbed the first handle I encountered: a cast iron frying pan. Hefting it like a caveman would do if he were holding a club, I pushed Jillian behind me and carefully stepped from the kitchen to the living room. My eyes widened with surprise. Sherlock had every right to be barking. The frying pan slipped from my fingers and clunked heavily to the ground.

There was a strange person standing in the middle of my living room, wearing a black hoodie sweatshirt and black pants. The hood had been pulled up and for-ward, obscuring the intruder's face. Whoever it was had a gun pointed straight at me. A long, slender arm reached up to pull back the hood.

"Call off your dog or else the first shot is going right between his eyes," Taylor Rossen coldly informed me as the gun swiveled down to point at Sherlock.

ELEVEN

The gun cocked loudly in the still room. Jillian and I were staring down the business end of a Glock 19. Several things struck me right off the bat. First off, how did Taylor Rossen have a key to my house? I had the locks changed. Second, the gun she was holding was steady as a rock in her hands, suggesting she was quite comfortable with it, and, more than likely, had used it before. And third, a spine-chilling sense of dread had washed over me. That cold-hearted woman was prepared to shoot Sherlock. I could see it in her eyes. Sherlock, on the other hand, looked as though he was ready to take on the intruder and not think twice about it

"Sherlock, get back here. RIGHT NOW!"

Even though I have never had any kids, and hadn't ever had to use a "daddy" voice on anybody, apparently I nailed it on my first attempt. Sherlock froze in his tracks. The corgi, with his hackles still raised, reluctantly returned to my side. He continued to bare his teeth and snarl at our uninvited guest.

"How did you get in here?" I asked as I stooped to hook a few fingers through Sherlock's collar. "How did you get a key to my house?"

Just then I felt something buzz my butt. I nearly jumped out of my skin. Thinking it was a bug of some sort, I ended up doing something that could only be described as spanking my own ass. Twice. Jillian gave me such a concerned look that, despite the circumstances, I almost burst out laughing.

"What's so funny?" Taylor demanded. "And why did you just slap your butt?"

"It's nothing," I mumbled, sobering quickly. "Thought a bug might've landed on me." The two women stared silently at me. "I'm not a fan, okay? I don't like bugs."

Taylor shrugged, reached into her front pocket, and pulled out a ring of keys. She slid one of them off and tossed it defiantly at me.

"I guess I won't be needing that one anymore."

Jillian bent down to retrieve the key.

"How did you get a copy of Zack's house key?"

"That's Grandma Bonnie's old house key," Taylor sneered. "Once Mr. Clueless here changed the locks then that became useless. I needed the new key. This key, in fact." She selected a shiny new key from her key ring and unclipped it. She held it mockingly up to me.

"How did you get that?" I demanded. "I just had those locks changed. There's no way you could've gotten a copy. Wait…don't tell me. You're friends with the locksmith, aren't you?"

Taylor sneered, "What do you think? I've got dirt on just about everyone in town. That's what you get for living in this crappy little dump your entire life. Mick and I came to an agreement. He gives me a copy of every key he makes and I don't tell the cops about his secret profession: cat burglary."

"So you're the one who killed Zora's assistant," I accused. "You're the mastermind behind everything. But why? What did Debra Jacobs ever do to you?"

"Are you kidding me?" Taylor all but shrieked. The

Glock started to shake in her hand, which didn't make me feel any better. "She deserved to die! You have no idea how vicious and cruel Debbie was. My mother used to have her babysit me. That woman lived to see others suffer. Did you know that she used to encourage me and my brother to fight? It made her laugh. Trust me. She got everything that was coming to her."

"Is that why you did all this?" I incredulously asked. "That's why you stole the glass tiger? Just so you could get back at the lady who was mean to you during your childhood?"

It was Taylor's turn to stare uncomprehendingly at me.

"I can see that I've given you way too much credit. You think I organized all of this just to exact some revenge on the woman who had been mean to me when I was little? If that was my motive then I would have targeted my own mother. She was twice as mean as Debra Jacobs had ever been and is at least ten times smarter than you will ever be."

"What do you expect?" I snapped, growing defensive. "I never said I was a detective. I'm making this up as I go."

"I'd recommend sticking to your day job," Taylor nonchalantly told me, "but in a minute or two you won't have to worry about that anymore."

"How long have you been planning this?" Jillian asked.

"Ever since my mother informed me that she had been cheated out of her inheritance. If I didn't do something then I was going to watch all my dreams fade away. Lentari Cellars was my ticket out of here, don't you see? I had to do something."

"I thought Abigail wanted the winery for herself?" I countered. I couldn't picture Taylor's mom as a doting mother figure.

The gun, which had been shaking in Taylor's hand, suddenly steadied. She shook her head no.

"Of course not. She thinks she wants it for herself, but I can get her to sign it over to me."

I shook my head. "I don't know. She was pretty adamant about getting the winery from me. Downright bitchy, if you ask me."

"I wasn't," Taylor sneered.

"Your mom is bankrupt." I'm not sure why I said that. Probably not my best move.

Taylor stared at me with undisguised malice in her eyes. "And whose fault is that?"

"Yours?" I guessed. Hey, what can I say? I have an innate ability to push the wrong buttons.

"Aunt Zora," Taylor contradicted.

Morticia Addams? How did she fit into this picture? I was confused and I'm sure my face showed it.

"She was always the perfect one," Taylor snapped. "She taunted my mother mercilessly, flaunting her successes. Everything she touched made money. My mother wasn't as fortunate."

"Let me see if I have this straight," I began. "You arranged to have that glass tiger stolen from your, what is she to you? Great aunt?"

"She's just my aunt," Taylor corrected.

I gave Taylor a piteous look.

"You arranged to have your aunt's gallery robbed just because you are jealous of her success? How pathetic is that?"

"What are you doing?" Jillian hissed at me. "Why are you egging her on?"

"Because it's keeping us alive," I whispered back. "If you've got a better idea, I'm all ears."

"Aunt Zora needed to know what it felt like to fail," Taylor continued, beginning to pace across the living room.

"By killing her assistant—her friend—and stealing a priceless piece of art," I accused. "That ought to make you daughter of the year. Or niece of the year. Whatever."

"Shut up!" Taylor shrieked. The Glock was once more pointed at me. "Do you have any idea how much of a pain in the ass you've been? Thanks to you and Dog Wonder the police now have my DNA on file." Taylor pushed the sleeve of her sweatshirt up and showed me her right arm. It was bandaged.

"How'd you get hurt?" I asked, genuinely curious.

"She cut me with her nail file," Taylor ruefully told me, "and then pushed me into that wall covered by paintings. I put up a hand to brace myself, but I ended up touching a painting. Imagine my surprise when an alarm went off. I never knew Zora had motion sensors on all those paintings. Obviously Debra did. Do you know what she did? She smirked at me, as though she had won. Well, I had the last laugh, didn't I?"

"So you left that painting at the gallery?" I asked, confused. "Why didn't you take it with you? The alarm was already going off."

"I should have," Taylor hissed. "I was simply out of time. I figured I'd return for the painting the following day to buy it off Zora. By the time I walked back into the gallery, the painting was already gone. Zora told me that you and your dog had found blood on the frame and it had therefore been turned over to the police."

"How did you get that picture of me for the paper?" I asked. "How did you even find it? I don't think it was posted anywhere online."

"You might not have posted it," Taylor haughtily informed me, "but that doesn't mean someone else didn't."

"Who?" I wanted to know.

"Phoenix is a big city," Taylor smirked. "Once I knew where to look it was easy to find you."

"The paper published that picture nearly two weeks ago," I pointed out. "How long have you been stalking me?"

"Ever since I learned my grandmother left her entire estate to you," Taylor spat as she continued to pace.

"How long have you known that your mother wasn't going to inherit Lentari Cellars?" Jillian asked.

"From the first moment I found my grandmother's will," Taylor flatly stated.

"You searched the house," I guessed.

"From top to bottom," Taylor confirmed. "I found a copy of her will in her desk. It wasn't hard to find."

"I imagine that's when you found her gun?" I asked.

Taylor shook her head. "No. I swiped it months ago. Grandma never knew it was missing."

"What about the fingerprint?" I asked, growing angrier by the second. "How did you get a copy of my fingerprint on your notebook?"

"It was easy," Taylor said. She held her phone up and wiggled it in the air. "I looked it up. Transferring a print from one surface to another is far easier than you might think."

"Tell me how you got my fingerprint," I demanded.

"I never set eyes on you until the day we met in Jillian's shop."

Taylor smiled sweetly at me.

"Is that so? Try again, hot shot."

Confused, I glanced at Jillian, who shrugged.

"You're telling me we met before? Where? When?"

"You don't remember? You sure know how to flatter a girl, Zack. We were in Phoenix," Taylor said as she resumed her pacing. She held her arm up to her head and said in a falsetto, "Zachary Anderson! How could you not remember our first meeting?"

"I swear to you I've never seen her before in my life," I assured Jillian. "I have no idea what this mixed bag of nuts is talking about."

"I waited on you at Zenburger. Several times. I took that job there just so I could wait on your table."

"To get the glass he was drinking from," Jillian breathed. "That's how you got his fingerprints. That's dedication for you. How long did you have to wait?"

"I spent nearly six weeks in Phoenix," Taylor stated as she continued to pace. "It took nearly two weeks before they'd allow me to wait on a table by myself and then another four before I was finally able to get my hands on your water glass."

"How did you even know I've been to Zenburger?" I asked. "I only learned about that place earlier this year. I haven't been there that many times."

"I followed you there several times," Taylor sneered. "Have you always dined by yourself? Loser."

"He was recently widowed," Jillian angrily told her. "Sometimes it's preferable to be by yourself. Trust me, I've done the same thing myself."

"You were following me around in Phoenix?" I

asked, doing my best to quell a growing feeling of rage. "For how long?"

"I found you the day after I arrived in Phoenix," Taylor snapped. "I had to know more about the person who stole my inheritance."

"I didn't steal a damn thing from you!" I shouted. Sherlock added his barks to my outburst. "Your grandmother left her estate to me and my wife. I had nothing to do with it!"

"Yet you wouldn't sign the winery over to its rightful owner, would you?" Taylor screamed back. The Glock began to waver again.

"Of course not," I said, trying valiantly to infuse as much calm back into my voice as possible. "I've decided to reopen the winery in Samantha's honor."

"I'm afraid not," Taylor contradicted. "There has been a change in plans."

Her voice had become eerily calm. I decided it wasn't a good sign. I had to stall for time while I tried to figure a way out of this mess.

"What's your plan, Taylor?" I asked, pointing at her gun. "Do you really plan on using that thing? I don't think you want two murders on your conscience, do you?"

"I've already committed two murders," Taylor coolly replied. "Do you think two more will make any difference to me?"

"You won't get away with this," Jillian vowed. I could hear the fear in her voice. "There's no way you can cover this up."

Taylor scoffed and looked around the room. "Don't you get it? I already have! I'm the one that found a buyer for the tiger. I'm the one who took down the town bitch,

Debra Jacobs. Not one person has ever thought to point a finger in my direction. Why? Because I'm not a threat. Well, let the fools in this city continue to think so."

"What about the guy who helped you steal the tiger?" I asked, eager to keep Taylor talking. I still hadn't a clue how the three of us were going to get out of this, but I knew I had to do something. The only thing I could think of, at the moment, was to stall for time. Where the hell was Vance when I needed him? How could I get a message to him? I casually felt the front pocket of my jeans. I could have sworn I had slid my phone into my pocket, but it wasn't there. Did I leave it on the table? Or the kitchen counter? I had to find some way to call for help. "That Russian dude. What did he ever do to you?"

"Gregor?" Taylor scoffed. "Please. Do you know how easy it was to find someone willing to buy the tiger, no questions asked? That's the power of the internet, baby. Who couldn't use an extra five million? So, I needed help to steal the tiger. I needed an actual thief. The tiger was my backup plan in case for some reason we were unable to get our hands on the winery. I had a theft to plan and I needed someone that could pull it off. Gregor did a remarkable job, didn't he? He got into Aunt Zora's gallery and disabled the entire security system in less than two minutes. I just wish he would have deactivated the motion sensors on the paintings. Damn fool."

"Is that why you killed him?" Jillian nervously asked. "Because he didn't completely deactivate all of the security systems in the gallery?"

"He got greedy," Taylor answered, with a shrug. "I can't have someone trying to renegotiate their terms every thirty minutes. He threatened to take the tiger as payment so I got him to take a nap. A permanent one."

"By poisoning him with strychnine?"

"Are you writing a book?" Taylor demanded, growing angry. "Look, I don't know what I gave him, okay? It was clear, it was odorless, and it got the job done. My mother's gardener, back when she could afford one, kept a locked cabinet out in the shed. Only the pesticides and the poisons were secured in that cabinet. I don't remember which one I used. Gregor always carried his own bottle of water with him wherever he went, so I needed to use something that was colorless. I picked one at random. One tablespoon of that liquid, mixed into his water, did the job. The rest, as they say, is history."

"Am I the only one concerned that she's revealing everything?" Jillian whispered in my ear the moment Taylor turned away. "This can't be a good thing for us."

"It isn't," I whispered back. "Don't worry. We'll be fine."

"Fine?" Taylor repeated, turning back around and pointing her Glock at me again. "You're going to be anything but fine here in just a few moments. Now give me your phone."

"What do you want my phone for?" I hesitantly asked as I reached into my pocket.

"What do you think? I installed a top-of-the-line tracker app without your consent. I've been tracking you all across town. I've listened in on your calls, read your texts, and have even listened as you putzed around here. I know you and Nancy Drew here found the app." Taylor groaned aloud and her grip on the gun faltered. "I hate you, Zack. I hate everything you stand for. Why did my grandmother leave everything to you and your wife? Why did you have to move to town?"

Was I mistaken or did Taylor's voice suddenly sound a lot like a whine?

"This winery was part of my inheritance. My mother promised me that Lentari Cellars would be mine!"

"What about Gerald?" I asked. I saw a look of sheer rage pass over Taylor's face and instantly regretted mentioning her brother's name.

"My brother? My brother?! What does Gerry have to do with anything? He doesn't deserve a penny! That lazy, good for nothing hasn't worked a day in his life! Why should he get anything? I'm the one busting my ass at that newspaper. I'm the one who is actually making a living. Not my mother, and certainly not my brother. He lives to do her bidding. Well, this winery is mine. Mine, do you hear me? And with you out of the picture, I'll finally get what rightfully belongs to me."

"With me out of the picture, wouldn't the estate revert to your mother?" I pointed out, inexplicably eager to continue pissing this nutbag off. "Or do you plan on eliminating your mother, too?"

"I can handle my mother, now give me your cell phone."

Resigned, I glanced back toward the kitchen counter.

"What?" Taylor asked, holding the gun disturbingly steady in her hand. "Where is it?"

"Back there somewhere," I told her. "It's either on the counter or the table."

Taylor brandished her gun.

"Alright. Move. And don't try anything stupid."

I heard a siren in the distance. I didn't have that many neighbors living around me. Could it be Vance? Had he somehow deduced we were in trouble? I eagerly looked back through the living room toward the front entry. Taylor cocked her head. She had heard the sirens, too.

"Hurry!" she snapped, as she ushered us back to the kitchen. "Find your damn phone and give it to me!"

We reached the kitchen and I paled. My cell wasn't there. Where had I put it?

"Where is it?" Taylor demanded. "Where have you hidden it?"

"I didn't hide it anywhere," I protested, trying to hide the fear that was rising in my belly. It was strange. I'll be honest, I knew there was a chance Jillian and I could get hurt, and it scared me. But as soon as Sherlock was thrown into the mix, I became downright petrified. I couldn't let anything happen to him. I was becoming frantic. "Just take it easy, Taylor. It's gotta be here somewhere." I moved over to the sink and tapped the counter. "This is where I had it last. It's gotta be somewhere close."

What was the saying? Always in the last place you looked? The best hiding place was often out in the open and more than likely being overlooked. I frantically glanced around the room.

"You're stalling for time!" Taylor shouted. She pointed the gun down at Sherlock. "What do I have to do? Shoot your dog? You know I will. If I'm not holding your cell in five seconds, then that's exactly what I'm going to do."

The sirens were growing progressively louder. Jillian tapped my shoulder and, surprisingly, pointed at my butt. Preoccupied with my own search, I didn't notice. I had started patting down my pockets. Jillian tapped my shoulder again.

"What?" I snapped. I would later apologize for how rudely that had come out but thankfully Jillian, bless

her heart, had blamed my attitude on the less than de-
sirable circumstances we had found ourselves in.

"You've got something in your back pocket," Jillian
informed me. "It looks like either a flat narrow wallet
or else a cell phone."

I quickly reached into my back pocket and pulled out
a cell. I shook my head. I didn't even remember putting
it there. Whatever. A sense of relief washed over me.
Hopefully Taylor would take the phone and run. Those
sirens were close. They had to be less than half a mile
away and were closing rapidly.

A flash of color caught my eye. I looked down at the
phone I was holding. The smart phone was encased in
a blinged-out purple case. It was Jillian's phone. What
had I done with mine?

Then it came to me. I had set it down on the coffee
table as I walked by on my way to the kitchen. I flicked
my eyes over to the coffee table and sucked in a breath.
It wasn't there!

Confused, I looked over at Jillian. Her scared eyes
met mine. I could tell she didn't have it nor did she have
any clue where it was. If Taylor didn't have it, then that
could only mean...

I glanced down at Sherlock, who was already staring
up at me. Just then he ran his tongue over his chops. I
stared at the dog. You've got to be kidding. There was
no way I could tell Taylor that the dog ate it and keep a
straight face. What had Sherlock done with it? Had the
corgi somehow known the phone needed to be hidden?
How in the world was that even possible?

"Who have you called?" Jillian quietly asked. Unfortunately, Taylor overheard.

"He's called someone?" Taylor asked. She snatched

the phone from my hands and looked at the display. The screen had been dimmed, but it wasn't off. The screen brightened the instant Taylor touched the display. She glanced at it and let out a string of profanities that would have made a sailor blush.

"I haven't called anyone!" I protested. "I swear! I don't even know how that phone got in my pocket."

The display confirmed that the phone had been connected to a call for the last twenty minutes. I should also mention that it's about the same time it would take to get from the city hall to here.

"Who did you call?" Taylor shouted. The gun began to shake once more. "Whose number is this?"

"Mine," a new voice flatly declared.

Everyone whirled around to stare at the front entry. The door was wide open and a steady stream of cops were pouring through. Vance had drawn his gun and had Taylor lined up in his sights.

"Drop it, Ms. Rossen. It's over."

"Like hell it is," Taylor snarled. The Glock never wavered and, dammit, it was still pointed at me. "There's no way I'm going down and not taking him with me. Zack has ruined my life so the least I can do is repay the favor. I'll see you in h—"

Sherlock darted forward and sank his teeth into the first part of Taylor that he could reach, namely her left ankle. She screamed in pain and instantly switched targets, taking aim on little Sherlock. To this day I don't know what came over me. I rushed forward, knocked the gun out of Taylor's hand, and, for the first time ever, struck a woman.

Taylor's head snapped back as my fist smashed into her face. She flew backwards, slamming into Vance and going down in a jumble of arms and legs. Several of the cops who had come in with Vance quickly pulled Taylor to her feet and slapped cuffs on her.

"Citizen's arrest!" Taylor screeched as a trickle of blood flowed out her nose. "I'm placing Zack Anderson under citizen's arrest! You are all witnesses! He physically assaulted me!"

"I didn't see a thing," Vance contradicted as he rolled to his feet. He turned to his fellow officers. "Any of you see anything?"

"Nope."

"Nada."

"Nuh-uh."

"Take Ms. Rossen into custody," Vance ordered.

"Charged with what?" Taylor sneered.

"For the murders of Ms. Debra Jacobs and Mr. Gregor Stefans. For the theft of *Bengál*. And probably for a whole slew of other charges, but I think those should do for now, dontcha think?"

"You have no proof," Taylor fired back.

"We have his phone," Vance said as he pointed at me. "Our tech boys are dying to get their hands on it to see what else you might've done."

"You'd better pick up the locksmith, too," Jillian quietly added.

"Mick?" Vance asked, puzzled. "I know that kid. Seems to be a decent guy. What's he got to do with anything?"

"Taylor said he gives her copies of all the keys he makes," Jillian explained.

I pointed at Taylor.

"Check her pockets. You're going to find a key ring with all sorts of keys on it. She not only had a key to this place, but also a key to the new set of locks I just had replaced. Yesterday."

A female officer appeared and gave Taylor an obligatory pat down. The ring of keys was produced. Taylor's nose lifted high in the air.

"So you'll catch a two-bit cat burglar. Big deal. You still don't have any proof against me."

"I need your phone, buddy," Vance told me, stretching out a hand.

"It vanished," I returned, earning a smug smile from Taylor. "It's in the house somewhere, I just don't know where. Do you want to know where it is? Ask him." I pointed at Sherlock.

"Your dog took your phone?" Vance asked, unable to hide the skepticism from his voice. "Seriously?"

At that moment Sherlock trotted over to the far corner of the couch. He lowered his head so he could shove his snout under the couch and woofed. He pawed at the carpet a few times, as though he was trying to dig his way under the sofa. Then he pulled his head out, turned to look back at us, and barked again.

"What is it, boy?" I asked. I dropped down to my knees so I could peer under the couch. I should have known. There was my cell. Sherlock must have pushed it under there. I don't know how he did it, or when he did it, only that I was glad that he did. I ruffled the fur behind his ears as I sat back on my haunches to look at my phone. I wiped the display across my chest to clear off several drops of doggie drool. I held it up for Vance to take.

"That is one smart dog," Vance said as he dropped to one knee to take my cell and give Sherlock another friendly pat. "We should make you an honorary police dog, fella."

Sherlock panted contentedly.

"What about the tiger?" Jillian asked.

"What about it?" Vance wanted to know.

"Have you found it yet?" she asked. "Has it turned up anywhere?"

"No," Vance admitted. "Who knows what she's done with the thing. I don't know if we'll ever recover it."

"You won't," Taylor vowed as she was led out the door. "You'll never find it and I'll never tell! Do you hear me? I still won, Zack. I still won!"

"What a nut case," Vance murmured. He looked around the living room. "Is everyone alright in here?"

I nodded. "Yeah. We're all good. I'm confused, though."

"About what?" Vance asked.

"You. I didn't call you. I swear I didn't."

"I know you didn't," Vance told me. "I called Jillian."

"You did?" I asked.

"You did?" Jillian echoed.

"Yeah. I was gonna warn you about Taylor. A quick records check on her confirmed she had been arrested before. Several times."

"For what?" I asked.

"Embezzlement," Vance answered. "Apparently she's greedy. She's been fired from every job she has ever worked."

"Then how'd she get a job at the newspaper?" I asked, curious.

"I wish I knew," Vance replied.

"She did say that she had dirt on just about everybody," Jillian recalled. She had hooked her arm through mine and was holding on tight. I have to say that I didn't find the experience unpleasant.

"That'd be a first for me," Vance said, smiling. "Blackmailing someone for a job. What's the world coming to?"

"I just hope you can find the tiger and return it to its rightful owner," Jillian said. "I don't like how confident Taylor was in thinking it would never be found."

"She's probably right," Vance agreed. "The tiger could be anywhere."

I looked down at Sherlock, and for once, he wasn't looking at me. However, sensing he was being watched, the little corgi turned to look. His stump of a tail started wiggling. I smiled as a thought occurred to me.

"I think I can help you with that. I just might know where she stashed the tiger."

EPILOGUE

"THIS? THIS IS where you think the world famous *Bengál* has been hidden? You've got to be kidding, pal."

I had to laugh. It had taken a lot of convincing, but I had finally managed to persuade Vance to follow me to what I believed was *Bengál*'s hiding place. Vance and I both pinched our noses shut. It stunk in there.

We were standing in the middle of the one place Sherlock had barked at every time we had driven by: Fur, Fins, & Feathers. It was PV's one and only pet store.

"Why in the world do you think the tiger is there?" Vance had asked me an hour earlier.

"Look at it this way," I had explained. "Sherlock found Gregor's body in the winery. He found the picture of Bonnie and her family. He guided me to the photo albums in the attic. He found the blood on the painting. Every time we drive by the pet store he barks like crazy. I always thought he was barking at Harry's office, which is right next door, and I guess he still could be. It's the one place that Sherlock keeps barking at that I haven't checked out yet. I say we look there first. It's at least worth a shot, right?"

"It's just a pet store," Vance had complained. "There's bound to be something in there that would attract his interest."

Vance had been right. From the moment we both

stepped through the doors we both thought it smelled like something had died in here. For the most part, the store was clean. However, there was a strong stench of dirty mop water permeating the air, mixed in with the unmistakably pungent odor of canine feces. Some dog must be feeling a whole lot better.

"Something the size of *Bengál* would stand out in a place like this," Vance said as he looked around the store. "There aren't very many hiding places large enough to hide it."

I dropped Sherlock's leash so I could let him wander around the store. He looked up at me and blinked a few times.

"You wanted to come in here, boy," I told the inquisitive corgi. "Here we are. Have at it."

Sherlock promptly trotted over to several large bales of straw and began sniffing around the edges. A young pimply-faced teenager hurried over and inserted himself between the straw bales and us.

"Uh, sorry, man. These have already been sold. Look, if you need a few bales I know I can order some for you. Probably take a week or so. Whataya say? You interested?"

"No thanks," I said as I picked up Sherlock's leash. "We're just looking." I gave the leash a gentle tug to let Sherlock know I wanted him to check out something else. The corgi refused to be budged. He started pawing at the bale of straw.

"What's he doing?" Vance asked as he stared down at the dog with the comically short legs, pawing at a bale of straw that was easily ten times his size.

"I don't know," I admitted. "He won't leave this bale alone."

Vance stared at the bale for a few moments before he ran his finger along one of the strands of twine.

"What's the matter?" I asked.

"The twine has several knots in it. Almost like the twine had been cut, spliced, and then retied." The detective slid a multi-tool gizmo out of a leather pouch on his belt. He flicked open a blade and cut the two strands of twine holding the bale together.

"Hey!" the kid protested. "You can't do that! Those bales have already been sold!"

"To whom?" Vance dryly asked as the bale fell apart. "To a lady by the name of Taylor Rossen?"

Nestled within the bale was the famed *Bengál* I had heard so much about. The glass tiger's one ruby eye peered out from under a layer of straw. I began clearing away the debris covering the glass sculpture. Vance, on the other hand, was eyeing the sullen kid that now looked as though he was about to break down into tears.

"Care to tell me how this ended up in the straw bale?" the detective dryly asked as he reached into his back pocket to pull out a set of cuffs.

"It's not my fault!" the kid wailed. "She made me do it!"

"How?" Vance demanded, growing angry. "How in God's name did she force you to hide stolen property, kid? Do you have any idea of the trouble you're in right now?"

"She said that she'd turn my father in if I didn't!"

The kid had turned on the water works and was not ashamed to show it.

"Your father? Is he the shop owner?" Vance asked.

"Yes," the boy sobbed. "Please, you mustn't tell anyone."

Vance gave me a quizzical look. I shrugged. I didn't have a clue what the kid was talking about, either.

"What did your father do?" Vance gently asked. "I can't help if I don't know what's wrong."

"That lady said my father would go to jail if she ever told the police what my father had done. I don't want him to go to jail. He's all I've got left!"

I watched a frown form on Vance's face.

"Out with it, kid. What'd he do?"

"Dad accepted several shipments of supplies, but reported they never arrived," the kid sullenly explained. "Things were tight for a few months. The store needed those supplies, but we couldn't pay for them."

"When was the last time your father did this?" Vance wanted to know.

"Two months ago. Business has since picked up and he's promised he'd never do that again."

"How did Taylor find out about it?" I asked.

The kid shook his head. "I don't know. She came strolling in here like she owned the place and said she had something to store in here and that I couldn't sell it. She said if anything happened to that bale then she'd personally see to it that I'd never see my father again."

"Relax, kid," Vance told the teenager. "Your father isn't going to jail, provided he contacts that distributor to make things right. Neither are you. I will be checking in with him in the near future to verify he's paid what's owed; of that you can be certain."

"How much is that thing worth?" the kid asked, pointing at the glass tiger.

"Taylor admitted she had a buyer lined up that was willing to pay her a cool five million in cash," I offered.

"Five million?" the teenager sputtered. "Dollars? For that?? Wow."

While Vance phoned in the report that *Bengál* had been found, Sherlock and I wandered back outside into the fresh air. I was met with a sight that stopped me in my tracks. A scowl formed.

"Mr. Anderson."

It was Abigail. She wore a crisply pressed blue business suit this time. Her hair was still up in a tight bun and she was again wearing those huge bulbous sunglasses that made her face resemble a bug.

"Ms. Lawson," I returned, mimicking the cold, unfriendly tone she had adopted with me.

"I came to…well, I came to apologize. On behalf of my children."

I folded my arms across my chest and stared impassively at her.

"Is that so?"

"Look. I don't approve of what Taylor did…"

"You think?" I interrupted. "She killed two people, Abigail. She was ready to kill two more!"

"Are you insinuating I'm a poor mother?" Abigail snapped.

Sherlock looked up at Abigail and growled at her. The grouchy crone actually took a few steps back.

"Did you hear me say that?" I countered. "Look, Abigail. You don't have to apologize for your kids. They're adults. They can speak for themselves. I'll be honest and say that I don't want anything to do with either of them. Or you, for that matter."

Abigail bristled with annoyance. She opened her mouth for some type of angry retort when I cut her off.

"Look, you've said some pretty nasty things," I slowly began. "And I'm willing to…"

"I'm not sorry for anything that I said," Abigail snapped, cutting me off in mid-sentence. She reached into her purse and pulled out a familiar wad of papers. "I still expect you to do the right thing and sign over the estate to me. It belonged to my mother so it should belong to me. She had no business leaving it to you."

Well, I tried.

"Ain't gonna happen, lady. I've already rehired Caden…"

Abigail's eyes opened wide with disbelief.

"…and he's agreed to help me reopen Lentari Cellars. Thank you for your lovely offer, but once again I'll have to decline. The winery and the estate stays with me. I'm sorry you're having trouble coming to terms with that, but I do suggest you accept it and move on. Lentari Cellars belongs to me now and it's going to stay that way. Do you understand?"

Abigail stormed off in a huff. I looked down at Sherlock and rumpled the fur behind his ears.

"I guess she did, pal. She wasn't too happy, was she?"

"Hey, Zack!" a voice called out.

I looked up. The voice had come from the next building over.

It was Harry. He was holding a leash in one hand and a pizza box in the other.

"I thought that was your Jeep, buddy."

He also had the biggest smirk I had ever seen on his face. I had already noticed what was on the other end of the leash. So had Sherlock.

"Harry, there's no way, pal."

"Aww, come on. She needs a home, too. Look at you. You're a natural dog owner now. This little girl was dropped off at my clinic earlier today. She's a friendly little thing, although she's a bit shy. I instantly thought of you."

Sherlock pushed his way forward and touched noses with the newcomer. Harry had a second corgi with him. This one was red and white and was slightly smaller than Sherlock. The second corgi curiously inched closer and let out a snort. Sherlock took a small hop back, dropped down so his butt was up in the air, and barked a greeting. The new corgi mimicked him and yipped a reply.

"There, you see? They're already getting along great!"

"Harry, no! I already have one corgi and he's a handful. I cannot even begin to imagine what life would be like if I had two, so put that thought out of your mind."

My friend ignored me. He squatted down next to the small red and white female and draped an arm around her. Grinning, Harry finally looked up at me.

"See? I told you I'd find you a new home. Meet your new daddy!"

* * * * *

AUTHOR'S NOTE

I'VE NEVER WRITTEN such a short novel in my entire life. Short stories, sure, but a novel? I'm used to writing epic fantasy, where the average novel is 100,000+ words. I had just assumed that mystery novels were going to be the same length as the fantasy ones and didn't think twice about how long it'd be. That is, until my wife jokingly told me one day that I'd never be able to keep it under 90,000. In fact, this novel was only supposed to be 50-52K words. Why that number? I looked up many of the books that I'd like to be in the same genre with to get an average of the word counts. The vast majority were between 50-52K words, so I vowed to be the same. Well, let's just say I missed the mark. By over 10K. Hope you're not too mad at me. :)

For those of you that may be interested to know, Pomme Valley was inspired by a real life town in Oregon that is just as picturesque as I hope I've made it sound. Jacksonville. I did my research when planning this town. Maps, streets, businesses, people, etc. My wife and I spent an entire weekend determining which businesses the town has, where they're located on the map, who runs them, what they look like, and so on and so forth. I've got my PV binder right next to me that has everything I need to know about my fictional town. I'm toying with the idea of putting some of the information I've collected online. Maps, businesses, info about planned festivals, etc.

I also based Zack's experience with wine on my own. I can't stand the stuff, I don't like to drink it, and know next to nothing about it. That is, I used to know next to nothing. I've begun to make an active effort to learn more about what I'm writing about. No, I still won't drink it, but I am learning how it's made, the types of machinery used, etc. I even bought one of those education courses that promises to teach you all about wine and how it's made. I won't bore you with the details, but suffice to say I'm trying to get better.

Now for the question that I'm really hoping you're asking right about now. What's next? When can we expect to see another Corgi Case File story? Will the next book really be about a mummy? I've already started planning out CCF2 and I'm having a lot of fun with it. Let me give you a few details… A traveling Egyptology exhibit, a vanishing mummy, reports of seeing said mummy appear throughout town, a town on edge, and two corgis doing everything they can to encourage their daddy to take an active part in the mummy sightings.

If you liked the book I would ask that you consider leaving a review. Believe it or not, it really does help an author out. The more positive reviews that are out there the more noticeable an author becomes. Want to be certain you never miss out on a new title being released? Stop by the blog and sign up for the newsletter. Any time I'm running contests, or requesting character submissions, or preparing to release a new title, I'll send out a newsletter to alert the fans. Trust me, I don't send them out nearly as much as I should.

Again, thank you for giving my book a try. I certainly hope you enjoyed it. If you have any questions or comments about the book then feel free to track me down online and ask away! I always keep an eye on my blog and can also be reached on my Facebook account.

Hope to see you online!
J.

Jeffrey M. Poole is a professional author living in sunny Phoenix, AZ, with his wife, Giliane, and their Welsh Corgi, Kinsey. He is the best-selling author of fantasy series Bakkian Chronicles, Tales of Lentari, and the mystery series Corgi Case Files.

Jeffrey's interests include astronomy, archaeology, archery, scuba diving, collecting movies, and tinkering with any electronic gadget he can get his hands on. Fans can follow Jeffrey online at his blog: www.AuthorJMPoole.com

Get 3 FREE REWARDS!

We'll send you 2 FREE Books **plus** a FREE Mystery Gift.

FREE
Value Over
$20

Both the **Harlequin Intrigue®** and **Harlequin®** Romantic Suspense series feature compelling novels filled with heart-racing action-packed romance that will keep you on the edge of your seat.